Nouveau
Cahier du jour
Cahier du soir

3e

14-15 ans

Anglais LV1

W0363572

Auteurs
Nicole de Vannoise
Jean Cureau
Professeurs d'Anglais au collège

Auteur du mémento
Coline Segonne
Professeur d'Anglais au collège

MAGNARD

Présentation

Un cahier complet

- **Ce cahier d'Anglais, destiné aux élèves de 3e, est conforme aux derniers programmes.** Il reprend toutes les notions et couvre tous les domaines.
- **La rubrique « Observer et retenir »** propose toutes les **leçons** accompagnées d'**exemples**.
- **La rubrique « S'entraîner »** propose des **exercices progressifs** pour réinvestir les acquisitions. Ils sont classés par niveau de difficulté (de * à ***).
- À la fin de chaque page, l'élève est invité à **s'auto-évaluer**.

→ *Les corrigés détachables sont situés au centre du cahier.*

Un mémento visuel

Un mémento avec l'essentiel à retenir en Anglais 3e :
pour une mémorisation visuelle efficace !

→ *À détacher au centre du cahier et à conserver toute l'année.*

POUR LE CAHIER :
Illustration de couverture : Lupe Granité – **Illustrations intérieures :** Pénélope Paicheler – **Conception graphique (couverture) :** Yannick Le Bourg et Raphaël Hadid – **Mise en pages :** Facompo – **Cartographie :** Valérie Goncalves, Christel Parolini
Crédits iconographiques : © Hulton Archive/Getty Images pour la photographie de Nelson Mandela (p. 20)

POUR LE MÉMENTO VISUEL DÉTACHABLE :
Illustrations : Aurélie Verdon – **Mise en pages :** Linéale

Sommaire

VOCABULAIRE ET CIVILISATION

GRAMMAIRE

ANNEXES

Mémento visuel détachable

Corrigés détachables au centre du cahier

1 Les îles Britanniques et les États-Unis
The British Isles and the USA

→ Corrigés p. I

Observer et retenir

Les îles Britanniques

Les États-Unis

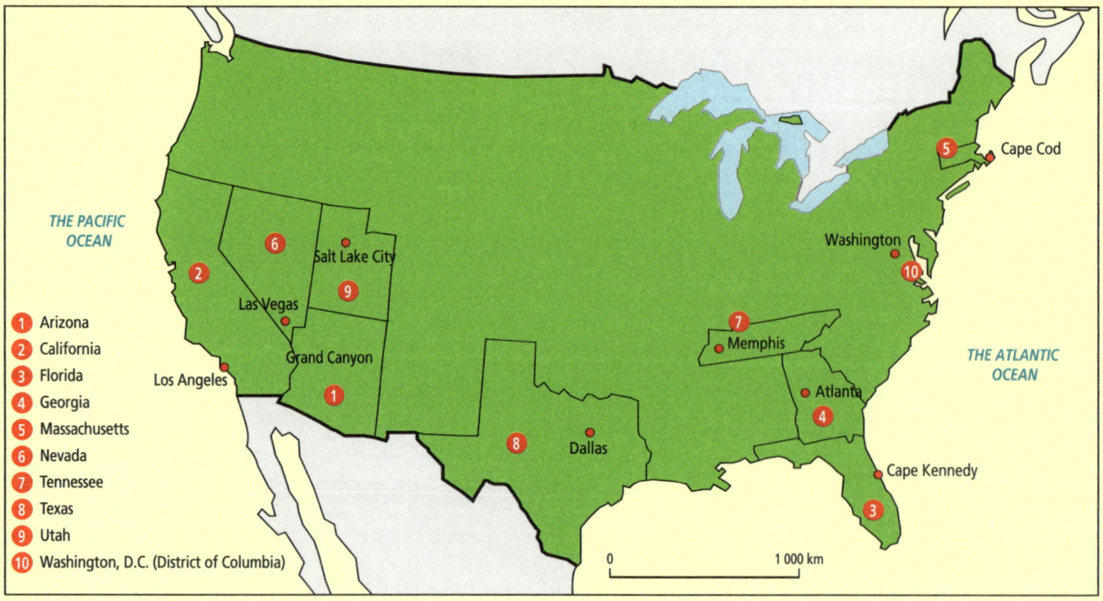

S'entraîner

1 ★ Voici les mers qui baignent les îles Britanniques : *the Atlantic Ocean* – *the Channel* – *the Irish Sea* – *the North Sea*.
Complétez les phrases ci-dessous.

1. England is washed by ....
2. Northern Ireland is washed by ....
3. Scotland is washed by ....
4. Wales is washed by ....

2 ★★ Écrivez les noms des villes suivantes sur la carte page 4 :
***Cardiff* – *Edinburgh* – *London* – *Oxford* – *Plymouth* – *Cambridge* – *Liverpool* – *Belfast* – *Dublin*.**

Aide
Elles sont signalées par un point orange et par leur initiale.

3 ★★ Chacune de ces villes est caractérisée par un mot dont les lettres sont mélangées. À vous de les rétablir.

1. Cardiff is the capital of AELSW.
....
2. Edinburgh is the capital of ACDLNOST.
....
3. London is the capital of ADEGLNN.
....
4. Oxford is famous for its CEEGLLOS.
....
5. Plymouth is in the HOSTU-ESTW of England.
....

4 ★★★ Complétez les phrases suivantes avec un des lieux indiqués par un numéro sur la carte des États-Unis.

1. The president lives in Washington: ....
2. Las Vegas, the capital of gambling, is in: ....
3. Hollywood studios are in: ....
4. Rockets are launched from Cape Kennedy in: ....
5. Kennedy was assassinated in Dallas: ....
6. The Pilgrim Fathers landed at Cape Cod: ....
7. Elvis Presley gave his first public concert in Memphis: ....
8. Atlanta is the capital of: ....
9. Most Mormons live and work in Salt Lake City: ....
10. The Grand Canyon is the most famous landscape in: ....

5 ★★★ Écrivez les noms des neuf États indiqués sur la carte des États-Unis suivant leur situation géographique.

in the North-East	in the South-East	in the South	in the West
....	....	....	....
....	....	....	....
....	....	....	....
....	....	....	....

Auto évaluation Très bien ☐ Bien ☐ Pas assez bien ☐

2 L'espace et le temps
Space and time

→ Corrigés p. I

Observer et retenir

A

The scene takes place in a rural area, in the twenties.

1 meadow
2 hedge
3 barn
4 daffodil
5 lily of the valley
6 poppy
7 sunset

B

Later on, a semi-detached house was built on the meadow; it was in the fifties.

1 fence

C

Nowadays, many country people have become town dwellers.

1 a three-storey building
2 an ad(vertisement)
3 towers
4 an aerial
5 a satellite dish

D

In fifty years' time, the men of Earth 1 will settle in space stations 2.

3 spacecraft
4 spaceman

S'entraîner

1 ★ Répondez aux questions suivantes.

1. Image A

a. What can you see in the bottom left-hand corner?

....

....

b. What is there between the meadow and the barn?

....

2. Image C

a. Where do town dwellers live in?

....

b. By which technical means do they receive TV programmes?

....

....

2 ★★ Comparez les images B et A en complétant les phrases suivantes.

1. In picture B, the cow ....

....

2. In picture B, the barn ....

....

3. In picture B, a semi-detached house ....

....

4. In picture B, a road ....

....

3 ★★ Complétez :

- les blancs en début de phrase avec l'une des expressions de temps suivantes : ***eventually*** – ***from now on*** – ***nowadays*** – ***seventy years ago*** – ***thirty years later*** ;
- les blancs en fin de phrase avec les mots de la page 6.

1. .... there was a farm in this ....
2. .... a semi-detached house was built on the ....
3. .... there are a three-storey building and higher towers for ....
4. .... there is not enough space on ....
5. .... earthmen will have to settle in ....

4 ★★★ Décrivez l'image D en 4 phrases.

1. ....
2. ....
3. ....
4. ....

5 ★★★ Écrivez un court paragraphe (100 mots maximum) sur le sujet : *Living in the country*. Votre texte devra comporter les mots suivants : ***barn*** – ***cow*** – ***farm*** – ***fence*** – ***lane*** – ***meadow***.

....

Auto évaluation — Très bien ☐ Bien ☐ Pas assez bien ☐

3 Les loisirs
Leisure

→ Corrigés p. I

Observer et retenir

A

The Six Nations Championship.

1. the **leek**
2. the **thistle**
3. the **shamrock**
4. the **cock**
5. the **rose**
6. the **flag**

B

"Have I got my **boarding card**? (1) my **insurance policy**? (2) Gosh! My **flight** is **delayed**! I'll be late."

Peter is a TV **addict**.
He is **glued** to the box all day long.

C

- I went **sightseeing** (1) from a **double-decker** (bus) (2).
- I took a train to Oxford (3).
- Now I'm **hitchhiking** (4).
- I'd like to hitch a **ride** to my **camp site** (5) or to a **bed and breakfast** (6).
- My **backpack** (7) is very heavy.

D

For my vacation:

- see my **travel agent** (1)
- buy a **plane ticket** to New York (2)
- **rent** a car (hope it won't be **damaged**) (3)
- buy a map of the **motorways** (to find the shortest **route**) (4)
- and a **suitcase** (5)

S'entraîner

1 ★ Êtes-vous un « accro » aux écrans ? Pour le savoir, complétez le tableau suivant et comptez vos points.

Do you watch…	every day?	once a week?	once a month?	never?
the news				
sitcoms				
serials				
reports				
films				
shows				
theatrical performances				

Points

Count 5 points for every day, 4 points for once a week, 2 points for once a month, 0 point for never. Add up all these numbers.

What's your score? from 25 to 40, you are a real screen addict.
from 15 to 25, you are a selective viewer.
from 0 to 15, have you got a screen at home?

2 ★★ Image A – Voici les symboles des pays qui participent au Tournoi des Six Nations. Écrivez le nom de chaque nation en face de son symbole.

1. the thistle ....
2. the leek ....
3. the shamrock ....
4. the rose ....
5. the cock ....
6. the flag ....

3 ★★ Image B – Complétez les phrases en choisissant les mots dans la liste suivante :
***board* (v.) – *boarding card* – *cancelled* – *delayed* – *fly* (v.).**

Dear Sally,

I wanted to .... to New York but my flight was ....

So I had to wait for two hours. Moreover I couldn't .... the next plane because I had lost my .... Then all the other flights were .... because of a strike. So I had no choice and I came back home.

Love from Peter.

4 ★★★ Images C et D – L'étudiant (*S* = *student*) et l'homme d'affaires (*B* = *businessman*) ne voyagent pas de la même façon. Expliquez les différences en répondant aux questions suivantes.

1. Where do they get their tickets?

S ....

B ....

2. How do they travel?

S ....

B ....

3. What do they carry with them?

S ....

B ....

4. Where do they sleep when they travel?

S ....

B ....

Auto évaluation Très bien ☐ Bien ☐ Pas assez bien ☐

4 Le monde du travail
The working world

→ Corrigés p. I

Observer et retenir

■ **A demonstration of workers, employees and unemployed people**

The chairman
↓
The managers
↓
Executives
↓ Foremen → ↓ Workers
↓ Employees

■ **The organisation of a company**

Peter was **sacked (dismissed).**

He had an interview at a **Job Centre** to apply for a job.

He attended a **training course** and got more efficient

and he finally got a job in a **reliable and successful company**.

S'entraîner

1 ★ Associez les phrases de la première colonne avec les personnes qui les ont prononcées (colonne 2) et les lieux dans lesquels elles ont été prononcées (colonne 3).

1. We have to reorganise our company.	a. trade unionists	A. at the Job Centre
2. We want higher wages.	b. a trainer	B. in the street
3. I'd like to find a job.	c. the chairman	C. in a demonstration
4. Do it again or you'll be sacked.	d. a photographer	D. at a training centre
5. I'm going to explain that.	e. a foreman	E. in his office
6. Just a second. Don't move!	f. an applicant	F. in a factory

2 ★★ Trouvez le contraire des mots suivants.

1. badly-paid → ....
2. jobless → ....
3. skilled → ....
4. on duty → ....

3 ★★ Entourez l'intrus dans chaque série de mots.

1. dismiss – fire – hire – sack
2. dole – income – salary – money
3. company – factory – firm – society
4. crisis – prosperity – strikes – unemployment

4 ★★★ Remettez dans l'ordre les phrases suivantes.

An interview at the Job Centre

a. CLERK: Here you are. See you again two months from now.

b. WORKER: I've just been dismissed from my factory.

c. CLERK: You could apply for a better job.

d. WORKER: For how long?

e. CLERK: So you're looking for a job. Are you skilled or unskilled?

f. WORKER: Can you give me an application form?

g. CLERK: Please, sit down.

h. WORKER: Unfortunately I'm not skilled.

i. CLERK: I think you should attend a training programme.

j. WORKER: And then?

k. CLERK: About two months.

1	2	3	4	5	6	7	8	9	10	11

Auto évaluation Très bien ☐ Bien ☐ Pas assez bien ☐

5 Famille et relations
Family and relationships

→ Corrigés p. I

Observer et retenir

Family relations

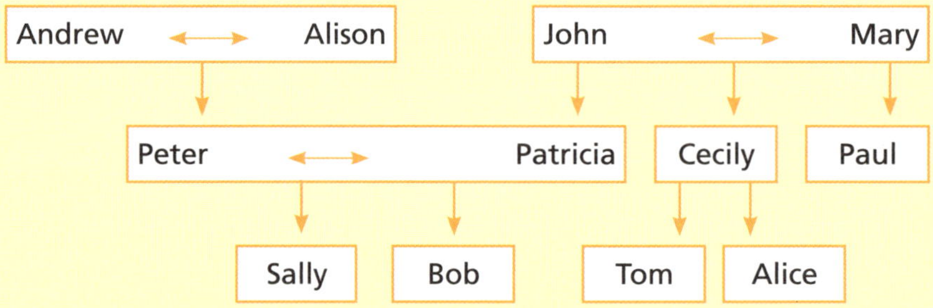

- Andrew is Patricia's **father-in-law**.
- Alison is Patricia's **mother-in-law**.
- Patricia is Andrew and Alison's **daughter-in-law**.
- She is Tom and Alice's **aunt**.
- Peter is Tom and Alice's **uncle**.
- Tom is Peter and Patricia's **nephew**.
- Alice is Peter and Patricia's **niece**.
- Cecily is a **widow**; her husband is dead.
- Paul is a **bachelor**; he is not married yet.

Behaviour and relationships

He is **prejudiced against** his sister… he doesn't know why.

Isn't he **aggressive**?

A **bossy** manager.

A **selfish** person.

At school

HEADMASTER – I was told you had **cheated**; you wrote exactly what your neighbour wrote.

STUDENT – That's what my teacher **pretends** I did. She **compelled** me to give my paper back immediately.

HEADMASTER – Right she was. Then you got **aggressive** and **threatened** your teacher with your ruler, didn't you?

STUDENT – It was just to **frighten** her; I didn't hit her… And she **persuaded** me to go and see you.

HEADMASTER – I **approve of** her because you **took advantage** of the situation to insult her. You seriously **hurt her feelings**.

STUDENT – I knew my lesson and she **prevented** me **from completing** my paper.

HEADMASTER – I suggest you go and **apologise** to her. If you don't **obey me**, you'll be severely **punished**.

S'entraîner

1 ★ À l'aide de la page 12, complétez les phrases suivantes en indiquant les liens de parenté.

1. John is Peter's ....
2. Sally is Cecily's ....
3. Patricia is .... aunt.
4. Mary is Peter's ....
5. Bob is Cecily's ....
6. Alice, Tom and .... are first cousins.
7. Paul is John and Mary's ....
8. Andrew and Alison are Sally and Bob's ....
9. Tom and Alice are .... grandchildren.
10. Cecily is John and Mary's ....
11. Cecily is Peter's ....

2 ★★ Quels mots de la page 12 correspondent aux situations suivantes ?

1. Make your bed, Sally – All right, Mum, immediately. ....
2. Stop it! Shut up, you bastard! ....
3. I was convinced by his arguments and I bought the car. ....
4. I'm only interested in my house, my computer, my dog. ....
5. He told me: "If you don't do what you are asked to, you'll see what happens." ....
6. She told me nasty words and I almost cried. ....

3 ★★★ Faites des phrases en utilisant les verbes indiqués. Respectez bien la construction de chacun.

1. apologise to (someone) for (doing something)
....
....
2. take advantage of *(+ noun)*
....
....
3. obey (someone)
....
....
4. compel (someone) to (do something)
....
....
5. suggest *(+ proposition)*
....
....
6. prevent (someone) from (doing something)
....
7. be prejudiced against (someone)
....
....
8. threaten (someone) with (something)
....
....
9. pretend *(+ proposition)*
....
....
10. be prejudiced against (someone) for (doing something)
....
....
11. approve of *(+ noun)*
....
....
12. Andrew showed (somebody something)
....
....
13. blame (someone) for (doing something)
....
....

Auto évaluation — Très bien ☐ Bien ☐ Pas assez bien ☐

6 Sentiments et traits de caractère
Feelings and psychological features

→ Corrigés p. I

Observer et retenir

absent-minded

clumsy

delighted

exhausted

nasty

puzzled

scornful

shy

stubborn

upset

sloppy

relieved

A dialogue between Jane – who is really fond of travelling – and her aunt, Betsy.

Jane – Auntie, I'm **keen on** travelling, you know.

Betsy – Where would you like to go?

Jane – To the States, of course. But it's too expensive. **I can't afford that.**

Betsy – I can't but **approve of** your choice, but…

Jane – Auntie, please, help me fly there.

Betsy – Well, Jane, **be sensible**! It costs a lot of money.

Jane – There are special rates for students.

Betsy – Aren't you **stubborn**! When you want something, you really want it.

Jane – I'm so **eager to** get there.

Betsy – I can't **blame** you **for** your obstinacy.

Jane – Auntie, I'm **longing for** spending my holidays there.

Betsy – Let's be positive. I promise you that if you pass your exam…

Jane – **Swear** it!

Betsy – I swear I'll pay for your trip if you succeed.

Jane – Oh, thank you, Auntie. I'm **looking forward** to that magnificent day.

S'entraîner

1 ★ Trouvez, page 14, les adjectifs évoqués par les situations suivantes.

1. What have I broken today? A glass, my watch, Auntie's vase…

....

2. Phew! Everything finally went all right.

....

3. He is not as clever as I. He's a good-for-nothing.

....

4. Glad the day is over! I couldn't do anything else.

....

5. Where are my keys? Where do I have to go?

....

6. What terrible news! I don't feel like eating anything.

....

7. …worn out pyjamas, a sock with a hole, a battered hat…

....

2 ★★ Complétez les phrases avec des mots ou expressions de la page 14.

1. When Mary saw a computer for the first time she stood .... in front of it.
2. He was so .... that he was always breaking things.
3. She didn't talk to anyone the first day of school because she was too ....
4. He was .... when he received the good news.
5. She wanted to buy a new computer but she .... it.
6. He is .... to the holidays.

3 ★★ Reformulez les phrases en remplaçant les mots soulignés par des mots ou expressions de la page 14.

1. Jane has not enough money to buy a computer.

....

2. She was very happy to go to the States.

....

3. She is very fond of travelling.

....

4. When she was young, she was very unpleasant.

....

5. Now she works very hard and feels very tired in the evening.

....

4 ★★★ Mots croisés.

1. embarrassed in front of people
2. extremely tired
3. looks down on others
4. enthusiastic
5. very moved
6. naughty and unpleasant
7. inattentive
8. careless and dirty
9. very pleased
10. awkward

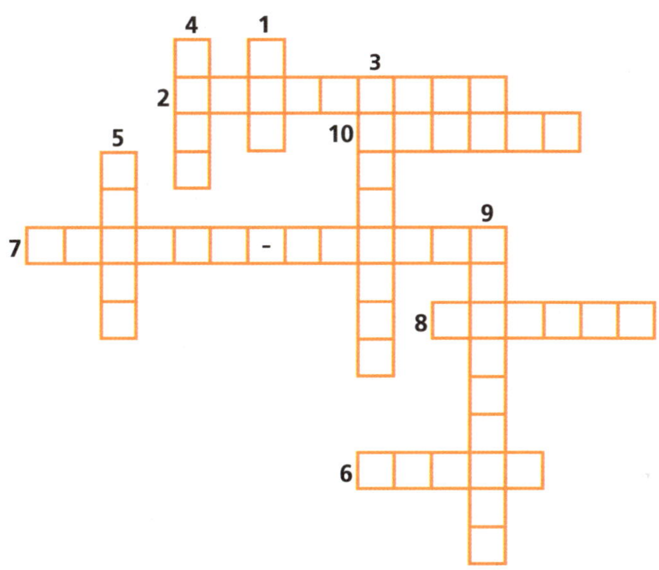

Auto évaluation — Très bien ☐ Bien ☐ Pas assez bien ☐

7 La nature et l'écologie
Nature and ecology

→ Corrigés p. I

Observer et retenir

Natural disasters

flood

earthquake

gale

heat wave

Other disasters

Fallout is fatal.
Ban the bomb!

A **leak** in the **tanker**
= an **oil slick**
on the sea.

A hole in the **ozone layer**
= the **greenhouse effect on the Earth.**

Nuclear waste
is a danger for
thousands of years.

Pollution and environment

- Acid rains ruin a lot of people in the world.
- Better not use sprays to protect the ozone layer.
- Using fertilisers can be dangerous for animals.
- The World Wildlife Fund protects endangered species.
- Carbon dioxide pollutes the atmosphere in towns.
- To preserve the quality of the air use lead-free petrol instead.
- Nuclear dumps must be buried deep in the earth.
- Detergents are used to dissolve oil slicks.

S'entraîner

1 ★ À chacune de ces définitions correspond un mot de la page 16. Trouvez-le.

1. place to leave one's rubbish
➜ ....
2. dangerous materials which are no longer used
➜ ....
3. something you spray on the ground to make plants grow better
➜ ....
4. a hole through which a liquid can pass
➜ ....
5. a thin sheet that covers and protects
➜ ....
6. a building made of glass in which plants grow
➜ ....
7. a soft dull grey metal
➜ ....

2 ★★ Effectuez une recherche sur Internet et répondez brièvement aux questions suivantes.

1. What is the most polluted town in the world? ....
2. What is the second most important nuclear power in the world? ....
3. What forest has been named "the Lung of the World"? ....
4. Can you name an endangered animal species?
....
5. Can you give the name of a famous oil slick?
....
6. What town in the States was severely damaged by an earthquake in 1906? ....
7. Where did a nuclear disaster occur in the eighties? ....
8. What are ecologists also called? ....

3 ★★★ Construisez des phrases contenant le mot indiqué.

1. flood ➜ ....
2. environmentalist ➜ ....
....
3. gale ➜ ....
4. heat wave ➜ ....
....
5. fallout ➜ ....
....
6. tanker ➜ ....
7. protest ➜ ....
....
8. ruin ➜ ....

4 ★★★ Écrivez trois phrases en faveur des centrales nucléaires (*nuclear power stations*) et trois phrases contre leur maintien et/ou leur développement.

1. For:
....
....
....
....
....
2. Against:
....
....
....
....

Auto évaluation   Très bien ☐   Bien ☐   Pas assez bien ☐

8 Les institutions
Institutions

→ Corrigés p. I

Observer et retenir

Governments

The United Kingdom

National anthem:

- "God save the King/Queen"
- The Queen reigns but does not govern.
- The **Prime Minister** governs.

The United States of America

National anthem:

- "The Star-Spangled Banner"
- The **President** governs.

The Parliament

→ **The House of Commons** (elected members called MPs = Members of Parliament)

→ **The House of Lords** (hereditary members or appointed by the Queen)

The Congress

→ **The Senate** (elected)

→ **The House of Representatives** (elected)

Elections

MPs are elected every 5 years.

Two main **parties**

→ **Conservative**

→ **Labour**

- Voting is a **duty** for every **citizen**.
- You must put your **ballot paper** into the **ballot box**.

- The President is elected every 4 years.
- The Senators are elected for 6 years.
- The Representatives are elected every 2 years.

Two main **parties**

→ **Republican**

→ **Democratic**

Justice

The **judge**

In a **trial**

Barristers are **lawyers** (specialists of the law). After listening to the **witnesses** and to the barristers (for the **defence** and for the **prosecution**) either the prisoner is declared **guilty** and **sentenced** to prison or not guilty and set free.

Religion

- For Christian people, **God** and **angels** ① are in **heaven**.
- The **Devil** ② is in **hell**.
- **Christians** read the Bible.
- **Jewish** people read and study the Torah.
- **Muslims** study the Koran.
- English churches are often surrounded by a **churchyard** ③.

④ a **cross** – ⑤ the **priest** – ⑥ the **steeple**.

S'entraîner

1 ★ Après avoir relu la page 18, trouvez qui a prononcé ces phrases.

1. This law should be passed.

....

2. I'm here to apply the law.

....

3. My client is not guilty.

....

4. I'll propose this bill to the Congress.

....

5. I've been sentenced to two years' imprisonment.

....

6. I study the Koran.

....

7. I'm glad my church is full every Sunday.

....

8. I must look up in my law books.

....

2 ★★ Corrigez les erreurs (soulignées) qui se sont glissées dans ces phrases. Barrez-les et récrivez les phrases correctes.

1. In Great Britain, the executives are elected for 2 years.

....

....

2. MPs are appointed by the PM.

....

3. On polling day, he put his driving licence into the letterbox.

....

....

4. As he was innocent, he was sent to prison.

....

5. The witness for the defence accused the prisoner.

....

....

6. Jews study the Bible.

....

3 ★★ Répondez aux questions suivantes.

1. In the UK, who is the Prime Minister appointed by?

....

2. How long is the President of the USA at the head of the nation?

....

3. In Great Britain, who defends the accused person on trial?

....

4. Who is asked to swear to tell the truth at a trial?

....

5. What is generally played before a rugby match starts?

....

6. What does a citizen do when he votes?

....

7. When is a person sentenced to prison?

....

4 ★★★ Décrivez l'image du paragraphe *Religion*, page 18, en complétant les phrases suivantes.

1. .... buried in a churchyard.
2. The priest is ....
3. In the top left-hand corner, ...
4. .... tombstones ....

....

5. .... by a fence.
6. Angels can be seen ....

Auto évaluation Très bien ☐ Bien ☐ Pas assez bien ☐

9 Deux personnalités célèbres
Two famous historical figures

→ Corrigés p. II

Observer et retenir

Martin Luther King

- Martin Luther King was born in Atlanta (Georgia) in 1929. He became a Baptist minister who preached **brotherhood and justice**.
- In 1955, he organised a **bus boycott** in Montgomery to protest segregation between blacks and whites. He also initiated peaceful protest marches **against racial discrimination**.
- He delivered a famous speech in Washington in 1963 entitled **"I have a dream"**. Thanks to his action, **the Civil Rights Act was passed in 1964**. The same year, he received **the Nobel Peace Prize** in Norway.
- He was assassinated in Memphis (Tennessee) in 1968. The USA decided to honour his memory on the third Monday of January each year. It is called **Martin Luther King Day**.

Help
brotherhood: *fraternité*
to initiate: *être à l'origine de*
to pass: *voter*
thanks to: *grâce à*

Nelson Mandela

- Nelson Mandela was born in South Africa in 1918.
- In 1948, the white power decided to separate the population into four groups setting the blacks apart: this segregation was called **Apartheid**.
- In 1955, Nelson Mandela, who had become a lawyer, initiated, through a charter, **a non-violent struggle against Apartheid**. Due to this movement, he was **sentenced to life imprisonment** in 1964.
- While Mandela was in prison, several **riots and strikes** took place in townships. For political reasons, **President de Klerk released him** in 1990 and asked him to cooperate in view to put an end to Apartheid. In 1993 they both received **the Nobel Peace Prize** for their common work.
- In his turn, Mandela was elected **President of South Africa** in 1994. He gave up his political activities in 1997. Then, his aim was to fight AIDS.
- He died at his home in Houghton in 2013. Today, he is extremely popular, honoured and loved by the South Africans who commemorate his action on **Mandela Day**.

Help
struggle: *lutte*
due to: *en raison de*
riot: *émeute*
strike: *grève*
to give up: *abandonner*
aim: *but*

S'entraîner

1 ★ Cochez le mot qui convient pour compléter les phrases suivantes.

1. Martin Luther King lived for .... years.

a. ☐ 42 b. ☐ 39 c. ☐ 50

2. He was a ....

a. ☐ lawyer b. ☐ preacher c. ☐ teacher

3. The Civil Rights Act gave racial ....

a. ☐ equality b. ☐ equity c. ☐ discrimination

4. It was the end of ....

a. ☐ racism b. ☐ segregation c. ☐ injustice

5. In his struggle, he organised ....

a. ☐ race riots b. ☐ non-violent actions c. ☐ street fights

6. He received the Nobel Peace Prize in ....

a. ☐ New York b. ☐ Paris c. ☐ Oslo

7. He was assassinated in ....

a. ☐ Tennessee b. ☐ Texas c. ☐ Alabama

8. The speech "I have a dream" was delivered in ....

a. ☐ Washington b. ☐ New York c. ☐ Boston

2 ★★ Complétez les phrases suivantes.

1. Nelson Mandela was born in .... *(country)*

2. After studying law he became a ....

3. The Apartheid began in ....

4. Mandela was imprisoned because ....

5. He was a prisoner for .... years.

6. Meanwhile, the blacks set up ....

7. In 1990 he was released thanks to President .... *(name)*

> **Remarque**
> Les éléments entre parenthèses donnent une précision sur la réponse à donner.

8. With President de Klerk, he was awarded ....

9. One year later, he was elected ....

10. Every year, ... celebrates his action. *(a special day)*

3 ★★★ Trouvez quatre points communs entre Martin Luther King et Nelson Mandela.

1. ....
....

2. ....
....

3. ....
....

4. ....

Auto évaluation — Très bien ☐ Bien ☐ Pas assez bien ☐

10 L'interrogation

→ Corrigés p. II

Observer et retenir

Absent-mindedness

BOB – **Whose** is that moped outside?
DAVE – A moped? **What** is it **like**?
BOB – It's all red.
DAVE – It must be Robert's. **Isn't he** absent-minded?
BOB – I agree. He'll take it tomorrow, **won't he**?
DAVE – I think so. But how will he go back home tonight?
BOB – He hasn't thought of it, **has he**?
DAVE – Forget him. Let's drive home, **shall we**?

L'ordre des mots

Vous connaissez déjà bien : ***who***, ***what***, ***which***, ***where***, ***why***, ***how much***, ***how many***, ***how long*** (durée), ***how often*** (fréquence)…

Interrogation	Interro-négation
Construction de base (Mot interrogatif) + aux./modal + sujet + base verbale ***Who*** *Who* (sujet) + forme verbale → *"Who broke this vase?" Clovis asked.* ***How much/many*** *How much/many* (sujet) + forme verbale → *How many workers demonstrated yesterday?* → *How much money were they given?*	**Construction de base** Aux./modal + *n't* + pronom sujet + base verbale → *Didn't I tell you yesterday?* ***Tags*** (reprises en fin de phrase) – Sujet + (aux./modal) + verbe… ; aux./modal + *n't* + pronom sujet + ? → *John will do it if asked to, won't he?* – Sujet + (aux./modal) + *not* + verbe… ; aux./modal + pronom sujet + ? → *Jane works for a newspaper, doesn't she?*

S'entraîner

1 ★ Posez les questions sur les mots soulignés.

1. Jane spoke to <u>Jim</u>.

....

2. <u>Bill's</u> moped is in front of the door.

....

3. He visits his friends <u>twice a year</u>.

....

2 ★★ Retrouvez les questions correspondant aux réponses qui vous sont données.

1. ....

John is tall, slim and fair-haired.

2. ....

Yes, he has already worked in a shop.

3. ....

Two years.

3 ★★ Complétez les phrases avec des *tags*.

1. You are a new student, ...?
2. You weren't a good student in your previous school, ...?
3. You can do better now, ...?
4. You love playing tennis, ...?

Auto évaluation Très bien ☐ Bien ☐ Pas assez bien ☐

11 Le présent

→ Corrigés p. II

Observer et retenir

For or against dogs

SARAH – Look! My old neighbour **is taking** her dog out.

LUCY – Poor dog, always in a flat. Dogs **need** space to be happy. **Do** you **know** that the number of dogs in town **is increasing** every year?

SARAH – Alas! My neighbour's dog **is** always **barking**. He is such a nuisance!

LUCY – Really? I **like** dogs. Is he here all the time?

SARAH – He barks every day at the same hour. Fortunately, she and her dog **are leaving** tomorrow. For a long month.

Présent simple	Présent en *-ing*
Sert à exprimer : – l'habitude → *He eats cereals for breakfast.* – l'opinion → *I think cereals are good for health.* – des idées générales → *Cereals bring a lot of vitamins.* – une caractéristique du sujet → *She lives as a retired person.*	Sert à exprimer : – une action en déroulement → *Look! He is eating his cereals.* – un point de vue (nuance d'agacement) avec *always* → *I'm fed up! He's always eating cereals!* – une idée de futur (décision prise) → *I'm buying a new car this year.*

Rappel
Il n'y a que deux temps simples en anglais : le présent et le *simple past* (ou prétérit).

S'entraîner

1 ★ Trouvez dans le dialogue ci-dessus les phrases exprimant les diverses valeurs du présent et écrivez-les.

1. une habitude → ....
....
2. une opinion → ....
....
3. une idée générale → ....
....
4. une action en déroulement → ....
....
5. un point de vue (irrité) → ....
....

2 ★★ Complétez les phrases suivantes soit avec un présent simple, soit avec un présent en *-ing*.

1. She *(go)* .... to the seaside every summer.
2. She *(always/cry)* .... She *(get)* .... on my nerves.
3. He generally *(sing)* .... in English but today he *(sing)* .... in French.
4. Listen! The baby *(cry)* ....

3 ★★★ Sur une feuille à part, traduisez les phrases suivantes.

1. Le nombre de skieurs augmente chaque année.
2. Les pistes deviennent de plus en plus encombrées.
3. Tu te plains toujours. Moi, je pars pour la Suisse demain.
4. L'eau bout. Sers-nous du thé. J'aime l'heure du thé.

Auto évaluation — Très bien ☐ Bien ☐ Pas assez bien ☐

12 Le passé

→ Corrigés p. II

Observer et retenir

Memories

He **came** in, **sat** down and **helped** himself with an orange juice. He **didn't know** what to do.

He **looked** out of the window. Mary **was walking** across the park. Mary… Ten years ago he **went** to America and **met** her… He **switched** on the television… While he **was watching** it, Fred **burst** in.

"How are you? Peter **told** me you **weren't** well. What can I do for you? Do you want me to stay with you?"

A dead silence. As usual James **was not answering** any questions. What a strange person! But James **was thinking**: "When I **was** a child I **lived** in New York and Mary… If only I **were** young again…"

■ Le ***simple past*** marque une rupture avec le présent et sert à exprimer **l'objectivité dans un récit** (**ex. :** *he came in, sat down and…*). Il peut être **daté** :

– de façon explicite par un **marqueur de temps** (**ex. :** *ten years ago, he went to America*) ;

– de façon implicite par le **contexte** (**ex. :** *when I was a child, I lived…*).

Rappel

Le *simple past* peut s'employer :
– dans le discours indirect ;
– dans les hypothèses (voir p. 29).

■ Le ***simple past* en *-ing*** sert à exprimer :

– une **action en déroulement** (**ex. :** *Mary was walking across the park*) ;

– un **point de vue** nuancé d'irritation (**ex. :** *He wasn't answering any questions*).

■ **Construction *simple past* en *-ing* + *simple past***

While he was watching TV, Fred burst in.

past en *-ing*	*simple past*
action en déroulement	évènement brusque, interruption

S'entraîner

1 ★ Utilisez le *simple past* ou le *simple past* en *-ing* pour compléter ces phrases.

When Mary *(hear)* …………………… the explosion, she *(go)* …………………… to the window. A car *(burn)* ……………………, people *(run)* …………………… here and there. She *(turn back)* …………………… and *(go out)* ……………………. She *(run)* …………………… downstairs when somebody *(bump)* …………………… into her. She *(fall)* …………………… down and *(shout)* ……………………. She *(live)* …………………… one of the worst moments of her life.

2 ★★ Mettez les phrases suivantes au discours indirect.

1. "You look tired", Mary said to James.

Mary said to James that ……………………………………

2. James answered: "I'm all right. I feel much better."

James answered that ……………………………………

……………………………………………………

3. Mary insisted and asked: "Why are you always lying?"

Mary asked him ……………………………………

3 ★★★ *"The Men of Earth came to Mars". What happened? On a sheet, tell the story in 100 words.*

Auto évaluation Très bien ☐ Bien ☐ Pas assez bien ☐

13 Present perfect

→ Corrigés p. II

Observer et retenir

Painting

A FRIEND – What **have** you **been doing**? I'm sure you'**ve been painting** again.

PAINTER – I'**ve been painting** for two hours.

A FRIEND – **Have** you **finished** your landscape?

PAINTER – Yes, I'**ve** just **painted** the last tree.

A FRIEND – I'**ve** also **painted** in my life. But I can't do it any more. I'**ve got** bad eyes now.

■ Le ***present perfect*** **(*have* + participe passé)** s'utilise pour parler :

– d'un **évènement non daté** du passé (**ex. :** *I've read a lot of books*) ;

– du **bilan** dans le **présent** d'une **action passée** (**ex. :** *I've read a lot of books and I can talk about them*) ;

– d'un **évènement commencé** dans le passé (**ex. :** *I haven't seen him for months*).

Astuce

Dans une phrase au *present perfect*, on peut trouver des adverbes tels que : ***just***, ***always***, ***ever***, ***never***, ***yet***.

■ Le ***present perfect* en *-ing*** s'utilise pour montrer :

– qu'une **activité commencée** dans le passé **se poursuit** au moment où l'on parle (**ex. :** *I've been living here for two years*) ;

– que l'on **s'intéresse à l'activité** plus qu'au résultat (**ex. :** *What have you been doing?*) ;

– une certaine **irritation** (**ex. :** *You've been smoking again!*).

S'entraîner

1 ★★ **Après avoir relu la fiche 12, complétez les phrases en utilisant le *simple past*, le *simple past* en *-ing*, le *present perfect* ou le *present perfect* en *-ing*.**

1. Mary *(apply)* .... for a job a week ago.
2. You *(eat)* .... chocolate: there are stains on your hands.
3. He *(look)* .... at the sea, when he *(see)* .... a dolphin.
4. Though the sun *(shine)* .... , he was not optimistic.
5. I *(clean)* .... the house this morning; now I can rest.
6. I *(not write)* .... any Xmas cards yet.
7. I'm sure I *(read)* .... this book one day but I *(forget)* .... the name of its author.
8. I couldn't sleep because my neighbours *(sing)* .... all night long.

2 ★★★ **Sur une feuille à part, traduisez les phrases suivantes.**

1. Il n'a pas encore trouvé l'appartement idéal.
2. Il en a visité six la semaine dernière.
3. On a fumé ici. Ouvrez la fenêtre !
4. Il pensait à elle. Elle rêvait de lui. Ils se sont enfin rencontrés la semaine dernière.
5. Combien de tasses de café as-tu bues aujourd'hui ?

Help

Traduisez « on » par *somebody*.

Auto évaluation Très bien ☐ Bien ☐ Pas assez bien ☐

14 Past perfect

→ Corrigés p. II

Observer et retenir

The burglar

It would be easy to come in. He **had stolen** the keys the day before. It was almost dark now. He **had been waiting** until the street was desert. He **had** carefully **planned** his crime. Rob **had told** him to bring a big bag. Here it was. He came in, stole all the jewels and silently shut the door when he went out. But he realized he **had forgotten** the bag and the keys inside! What an absent-minded burglar!

■ ***Had* + participe passé du verbe**

- En règle générale, le *past perfect* marque une **antériorité** par rapport à un **évènement révolu du passé**.

Exemple *He had stolen the keys* *the day before*.

- Il s'utilise aussi au discours rapporté : *he realised he had forgotten his bag.*

Il peut être accompagné des adverbes : ***just***, ***yet***, ***never***, ***always***, etc.

■ ***Had* + participe passé + (*be* + *-ing*)**

Les valeurs d'emploi sont les mêmes que pour le *present perfect*, mais dans le révolu.

Exemple *He had been waiting until...*

S'entraîner

1 ★★ Utilisez le *past perfect* ou le *simple past* dans l'histoire suivante.

When Peter *(arrive)* .... at the station he *(realise)* .... that he *(forget)* .... his wife's birthday. It was something that *(never happen)* .... before. He *(grasp)* .... the phone she *(offer)* .... him a few weeks before. She *(ask)* .... him to always carry it. He *(try)* .... to call her and *(remember)* .... that he *(not ask)* .... her where she was spending her afternoon. He *(never feel)* .... so ill-at-ease.

2 ★★ Mettez les phrases suivantes au discours indirect.

1. Mary asked John: "Why haven't you answered my letter?"

Mary asked John ....

2. John said: "I've already answered your letter."

John told her ....

3. Mary complained: "I've been waiting for it for ages."

Mary complained ....

3 ★★★ Traduisez les phrases suivantes.

1. J'avais déjà acheté ma voiture quand je me suis aperçu qu'elle était abîmée.

....

....

2. J'avais rêvé de cette voiture pendant des années.

....

3. Mon ami m'avait dit que c'était la meilleure.

....

Auto évaluation Très bien ☐ Bien ☐ Pas assez bien ☐

15 Ago, for, since

→ Corrigés p. II

Observer et retenir

■ ***Ago*** précise une rupture avec le temps présent. Il est accompagné d'un ***simple past***.
Ex. : *I applied for this job six months ago.*

■ ***For*** indique toujours une durée. Il peut être accompagné :
– d'un ***simple past*** → durée dans une période révolue (**ex. :** *Mr Smith worked in this factory for ten years*) ;
– d'un ***present perfect*** → bilan dans le présent (**ex. :** *Ms Tery has been a secretary for six months*) ;
– d'un ***past perfect*** → bilan dans le passé (**ex. :** *Ms Tery had studied typing for two years when she was hired*).

■ ***Since*** indique toujours le point de départ d'une activité.
Il est accompagné :
– d'un ***present perfect*** → bilan dans le présent (**ex. :** *Ms Tery has been working since September*) ;
– d'un ***past perfect*** → bilan dans le passé (**ex. :** *She had studied typing since 2004 when she was hired*).

Remarque
On peut combiner les idées de bilan et de durée à l'aide du ***present perfect*** (ou du ***past perfect***) + ***-ing***.
→ *He has been waiting for two hours, since midday.*

S'entraîner

1 ★★ Complétez les phrases suivantes avec *for* ou *since* dans la 1re colonne, ou *ago* dans la 2de.

	for, since		ago
1. I haven't slept well		several weeks	
2. Last year she travelled in Africa		two months	
3. This trip took place		six months	
4. His wife's parents have been married		1970	
5. In 1990 they had been married		twenty years	
6. Jane has been dreaming of getting married		ages	

2 ★★★ À partir de cette biographie de David Lodge, traduisez le texte suivant.

1935 birth → 1955 1st degree → national service → 1959 2nd degree → literature teacher → 1987 retirement → novelist → 2018

1. David Lodge est né il y a quatre-vingt-trois ans.

....

2. Il écrit des romans depuis 1960.

....

3. Il enseigna la littérature pendant vingt-sept ans.

....

4. Il habite Birmingham depuis cinquante-huit ans.

....

Auto évaluation Très bien ☐ Bien ☐ Pas assez bien ☐

16 L'expression du futur

→ Corrigés p. II

Observer et retenir

A strike?

FOREMAN – Work **stops** at five. I'm sure all the workers **are going to** meet.

PERSONNEL MANAGER – What's **going** to happen?

FOREMAN – They'**ll** probably **go** on strike.

P.M. – In fact there have been a lot of talks today.

FOREMAN – Really? So they **are going to** stop working for a week at least.

P.M. – Sorry. I have to leave you. I'**m having** an appointment with the director of the Work Standards Company.

FOREMAN – Hurry up then! The workers **are about to** go out.

P.M. – Goodbye. I'**ll jump** into my car.

Présent simple	Présent en *-ing*	*Be going to*	*Will*	*Be about to*
a. planning officiel	**b.** planning personnel	**c.** prédiction à partir d'indices	**d.** décision immédiate **e.** prédiction	**f.** imminence

Exemples

a. *Summer holidays begin on the 1st of July.*
b. *So I'm going on holiday on the 1st of July.*
c. *Worse than today. Dark grey clouds. It's going to rain.*
d. *Wait a minute! I'll answer. Hello…*
e. *Excuse me… Well, I hope the weather will be fine.*
f. *Still one minute. The race is about to start.*

S'entraîner

1 ★ Relisez le dialogue ci-dessus. Attribuez à chaque forme verbale sa valeur de futur. Utilisez les lettres du tableau.

1. stops → .... – 2. are going (to meet) → .... 3. is going (to happen) → .... – 4. They'll... go → .... – 5. are going to stop → .... – 6. I'm having → .... – 7. are about → .... – 8. I'll jump → ....

2 ★★ Complétez avec *will* ou *be going to*.

1. Listen! He .... speak.
2. You .... find the solution in this dictionary.
3. One day machines .... replace workmen in all the factories.
4. Look at his muscles! He .... be a boxer.

3 ★★★ Notez pour chaque phrase la forme verbale exprimant le futur (présent simple, présent en *-ing*, *be going to*, *will*, *be about to*), puis traduisez.

1. Vite, un verre d'eau ! Il va s'évanouir !
....
2. Si vous faites du hors-piste, vous déclencherez une avalanche.
....
....
3. Il fait trop chaud ici. Je vais ouvrir une fenêtre.
....
....
4. D'après l'horaire, l'avion décollera à 17 heures.
....
....

Auto évaluation — Très bien ☐ Bien ☐ Pas assez bien ☐

17 La condition, l'hypothèse

→ Corrigés p. II

Observer et retenir

Let's be prudent!

INSTRUCTOR – **If** there **is** a black flag, you **mustn't** ski. Understand?

SKIER – Yes, **if** there **is** a black flag, I **won't** ski.

INSTRUCTOR – Right. **If** the weather **got** better, I **would tell** you.

SKIER – Thank you. **If** I **have** the time, I**'ll go** and see you.

INSTRUCTOR – Remember last week. **If** the three youths **had looked** at the notice board, they **wouldn't be** dead today.

SKIER – Certainly. **If** they **had had** more information, they **wouldn't have been killed** by the avalanche.

	Temps/aspect de la principale	Temps/aspect de la subordonnée	Valeur
a.	présent simple	présent simple	conséquence immédiate
b.	présent simple	*will* + base verbale	conséquence à venir
c.	*simple past*	*would* + base verbale	irréel du présent
d.	*past perfect*	*would* + *have* + participe passé	irréel du passé

a. *If* pourrait être remplacé par *when*. La réalisation est automatique.

Exemple *If there is a will, there is a way.* → Si on veut, on peut.

b. La réalisation est possible dans l'avenir.

c. La réalisation est plus problématique mais pas exclue.

d. La réalisation est impossible. C'est le domaine du regret.

S'entraîner

1 ★ Relisez le dialogue ci-dessus et indiquez la valeur de chaque phrase ci-dessous en utilisant les lettres du tableau.

1. If the weather got better, I would tell you. ......
2. If I have the time, I'll go and see you. ......
3. If they had looked at the notice board, they wouldn't be dead. ......
4. If they had had more information, they wouldn't have been killed by the avalanche. ......

2 ★★ Complétez les phrases suivantes en mettant le verbe entre parenthèses au temps/aspect voulu.

1. If he .... his umbrella, he wouldn't have got wet. *(take)*
2. If I go to London, I .... the Tower. *(visit)*
3. If I had his phone number, I .... him. *(call)*
4. If the lights are red, cars .... *(stop)*
5. If they .... him, he would come. *(invite)*
6. The cat .... if the door had been closed. *(not go out)*

3 ★★★ Complétez ces phrases à votre convenance, en respectant la concordance des temps/aspects.

1. If I met a burglar in my flat, ...
2. If he doesn't tell the truth, ...
3. If someone bought my flat, ...
4. ...., I won't speak to him.

Auto évaluation Très bien ☐ Bien ☐ Pas assez bien ☐

18 Souhaits et regrets

→ Corrigés p. II

Observer et retenir

Wishes and regrets

Three wishes only…
I wish I had a good meal…
… and here was the best meal.
If only I had nice clothes…
… and she got splendid dresses.

I wish my son would stand by me…
… and here was her son standing by her.
… **And a lot of regrets!**
Silly me!

If only I had asked for a lot of money!
I wish I hadn't spoilt my three wishes!
I'd rather have asked for health and love.

Souhaits

Pour exprimer un souhait, on commence sa phrase par *I'd like*, *I wish* ou *I'd rather*.

- ***I'd like*** + nom/pronom objet + *to* + base verbale
  Exemple *I'd like my son to work better.*
- ***I wish*** + nom/pronom sujet + prétérit modal ou : *would* + b. v.
  Exemple *I wish my son worked better would work better.*
- ***I'd rather*** + nom/pronom sujet + prétérit modal
  Exemple *I'd rather he didn't waste his time.*

Attention
Le « prétérit modal » de *be* est *were*. On le trouve dans l'hypothèse (*suppose he were in the States now*) et dans les souhaits (*I wish I were a little richer*).

Regrets

Les regrets appartiennent au passé. Ils se rendent soit par un ***past*** (dit modal), soit par un ***past perfect*** (dit modal).

- Regrets dans le **présent** : *I wish he **had** more time to study.*
- Regrets dans le **passé** : *I wish/If only he **had worked** better when he was a student.*

S'entraîner

1 ★ Pour chaque phrase, indiquez si l'on rend compte d'une activité réelle (R) ou irréelle (I).

1. I wish I were abroad. ....
2. He wished them good luck. ....
3. I wish I hadn't eaten so much. ....
4. If he came by train, he would arrive earlier. ....
5. As he came by plane, he arrived late. ....

2 ★★ Traduisez les phrases suivantes.

1. I wish my son would work better.

....

2. If only I had more time to study.

....

3. I wish he hadn't given up his studies.

....

4. I'd rather have asked for health and love.

....

3 ★★★ Reformulez les phrases suivantes sous forme de souhaits.

1. Please, stop smoking.

....

....

2. I'm sorry you can't play the piano.

....

....

Auto évaluation — Très bien ☐ Bien ☐ Pas assez bien ☐

Nouveau Cahier du jour Cahier du soir

Corrigés

VOCABULAIRE ET CIVILISATION

1 Les îles Britanniques et les États-Unis — p. 5

1 1. the North Sea, the Channel, the Irish Sea – 2. the Irish Sea, the Atlantic Ocean – 3. the North Sea, the Atlantic Ocean, the Irish Sea – 4. the Atlantic Ocean, the Irish Sea.

2 Vérifiez sur un atlas ou votre livre de géographie.

3 1. Wales – 2. Scotland – 3. England – 4. colleges – 5. South-West.

4 1. Washington D.C. – 2. Nevada – 3. California – 4. Florida – 5. Texas – 6. Massachusetts – 7. Tennessee – 8. Georgia – 9. Utah – 10. Arizona.

5 In the North-East: Massachusetts, Washington D.C. – In the South-East: Florida, Georgia, Tennessee – In the South: Texas – In the West: Arizona, California, Nevada, Utah.

2 L'espace et le temps — p. 7

1 1. a. I can see a daffodil, a lily of the valley, a poppy. – b. There is a hedge. – 2. a. They live in buildings. – b. Through an aerial or thanks to a satellite dish.

2 1. is in the meadow behind the fence. – 2. has been destroyed. – 3. has been built on the meadow. – 4. has replaced the hedge.

3 *Corrigé suggéré :* 1. Seventy years ago there was a farm in this meadow. – 2. Thirty years later, a semi-detached house was built on the meadow. – 3. Nowadays, there are a three-storey building and higher towers for town-dwellers. – 4. From now on there is not enough space on Earth. – 5. Eventually earth-men will have to settle in space stations.

4 *Corrigé suggéré :* 1. In the bottom left-hand corner we can see the Earth. – 2. A spacecraft is flying to the space station. – 3. A spaceman is floating in the air. – 4. Above the spaceman, there is a planet.

5 *Corrigé suggéré :* Deborah and her husband David live on a farm. Close to the farmhouse they keep the hay in a barn to feed the cows in winter. Behind the house a lane leads to a meadow surrounded by a fence where cows graze in summer. Deborah and David enjoy living and working there.

3 Les loisirs — p. 9

1 Les réponses au test dépendent de vous !

2 1. Scotland – 2. Wales – 3. Ireland – 4. England – 5. France – 6. Italy.

3 fly – delayed – board – boarding card – cancelled.

4 1. The student gets them at the train station or at the bus station. The businessman gets them at his travel agency. – 2. The student usually hitchhikes or walks. The businessman rents a car and drives it. – 3. The student carries a backpack. The businessman carries a suitcase. – 4. The student sleeps under a tent in a camp site or at a bed and breakfast. The businessman stays in a hotel.

4 Le monde du travail — p. 11

1 1. c. E. – 2. a. B. – 3. f. A. – 4. e. F. – 5. b. D. – 6. d. C.

2 1. well-paid – 2. employed – 3. unskilled – 4. off duty.

3 1. hire – 2. dole – 3. society – 4. prosperity.

4 g. – b. – e. – h. – i. – d. – k. – j. – c. – f. – a.

5 Famille et relations — p. 13

1 1. father-in-law – 2. niece – 3. Tom and Alice's – 4. mother-in-law – 5. nephew – 6. Sally and Bob – 7. son – 8. grand-parents – 9. John and Mary's – 10. daughter – 11. sister-in-law.

2 1. obey – 2. aggressive – 3. persuade – 4. selfish – 5. threaten – 6. hurt my feelings.

3 *Corrigé suggéré :* 1. The guest apologised to the hostess for breaking a vase. – 2. She took advantage of the sales to buy herself a lot of clothes. – 3. Thomas obeys his master without barking. – 4. You aren't compelled to do it. It's up to you to decide. – 5. I suggest (that) we break for lunch now. – 6. Nobody can prevent them from getting married. – 7. He says they are stupid; he is prejudiced against the Martians. – 8. Jupiter threatened the humans with his flashes of lightning. – 9. He pretended he was the Master of the World. – 10. I was prejudiced against the Martians for speaking another language than mine. – 11. Paul's mother approves of his decision. – 12. Andrew showed Alice his photos. – 13. Lily blamed Emma for getting angry.

6 Sentiments et traits de caractère — p. 15

1 1. clumsy – 2. relieved – 3. scornful – 4. exhausted – 5. absent-minded – 6. upset – 7. sloppy.

2 1. puzzled – 2. clumsy – 3. shy – 4. delighted – 5. couldn't afford – 6. looking forward.

3 1. Jane can't afford to buy a computer. – 2. She was delighted to go to the States. – 3. She is keen on travelling. – 4. When she was young, she was nasty. – 5. Now she works very hard and feels exhausted in the evening.

4 1. shy – 2. exhausted – 3. scornful – 4. keen – 5. upset – 6. nasty – 7. absent-minded – 8. sloppy – 9. delighted – 10. clumsy.

7 La nature et l'écologie — p. 17

1 1. dump – 2. waste – 3. fertilisers – 4. leak – 5. layer – 6. greenhouse – 7. lead.

2 1. Kanpur (India) – 2. France – 3. the Amazon forest – 4. the blue whale/the white tiger – 5. Deepwater Horizon (Gulf of Mexico) – 6. San Francisco – 7. Tchernobyl – 8. the Greens.

3 *Corrigé suggéré :* 1. Thanks to his ark Noah survived the flood. – 2. Environmentalists want pesticides to be banned. – 3. The ship lost her mast in the gale. – 4. Every summer, Phoenix (Arizona) is struck by a heat wave. – 5. Lots of Japanese were killed by fallout in Hiroshima. – 6. Too many tankers clean their tanks too close to the shores. – 7. The Greens protest the massive use of fertilisers. – 8. The crops were ruined by the frost.

4 1. *For:* Nuclear plants generate the cheapest electricity in the world. It is a clean source of energy. 70% of French electricity is produced by nuclear plants.

2. *Against:* A nuclear power station's activity lasts only thirty or forty years. Nuclear waste can be active for decades; it can't be totally destroyed: it must be buried very deep in the earth. A radioactive leak may kill many people and endanger the environment.

8 Les institutions — p. 19

1 1. an MP – 2. a judge – 3. a barrister/a lawyer – 4. the President – 5. prisoner – 6. a Muslim – 7. a priest – 8. a lawyer/a barrister.

2 1. In the USA, the representatives are elected for two years. – 2. MPs are elected by the citizens. – 3. On polling day, he put his ballot paper into the ballot box. – 4. As he was guilty, he

Corrigés détachables

Corrigés détachables

was sent to prison. – 5. The witness for the prosecution accused the prisoner. – 6. Jews study the Torah.

3 1. He is appointed by the Queen. – 2. He is at the head of the nation for four years. – 3. The barrister for the defence does. – 4. Witnesses are. – 5. It is the national anthem. – 6. He puts his ballot paper into the ballot box. – 7. When he is guilty.

4 1. Dead people are buried in a churchyard. – 2. The priest is standing in front of the church. – 3. In the top left-hand corner, I can see the Devil. – 4. There are seven tombstones (surmounted by a cross) in the churchyard close to the church. – 5. This churchyard is surrounded by a fence. – 6. Angels can be seen in the top right-hand corner.

9 Deux personnalités célèbres ____ p. 21

1 1. b. – 2. b. – 3. a. – 4. b. – 5. b. – 6. c. – 7. a. – 8. a.

2 1. South Africa – 2. lawyer – 3. 1948 – 4. he took part in the struggle against Apartheid – 5. 27 years – 6. riots and strikes – 7. Frederik de Klerk – 8. the Nobel Peace Prize – 9. President of South Africa – 10. Mandela Day.

3 1. They struggled against racial segregation. – 2. They were sentenced to prison. – 3. They were awarded the Nobel Peace Prize. – 4. They are honoured on a special day.

GRAMMAIRE

10 L'interrogation ____ p. 22

1 1. Who did Jane speak to? – 2. Whose moped is in front of the door?/Whose is the moped in front of the door? – 3. How often does he visit his friends?

2 1. What is John like? – 2. Has he already worked in a shop? – 3. (For) how long has he worked in it?

3 1. aren't you? – 2. were you? – 3. can't you? – 4. don't you?

> **Attention**
> Ne pas confondre *what is he like?* (à quoi ressemble-t-il ?) et *how is he?* (comment va-t-il ?)

11 Le présent ____ p. 23

1 1. He barks every day at the same hour. – 2. I like dogs. – 3. Dogs need space to be happy. – 4. My old neighbour is taking her dog out. – 5. My neighbour's dog is always barking.

2 1. goes – 2. is always crying; is getting – 3. sings; is singing – 4. is crying.

3 1. The number of skiers is increasing every year. – 2. The tracks get more and more crowded. – 3. You are always complaining. I am leaving for Switzerland tomorrow. – 4. The water is boiling. Serve us tea. I like tea time.

12 Le passé ____ p. 24

1 heard – went – was burning – were running – turned back – went out – was running – bumped – fell down – shouted – was living.

2 1. he looked tired. – 2. he was all right and that he felt much better. – 3. why he was always lying.

3 *Corrigé suggéré :* The twenty Earthmen of the rocket landed on Mars in the dark. They stepped forward, stumbling on the rocks. Unable to see, they decided to sleep until daybreak. When, after a long period, they could see, they couldn't recognise each other because they were covered with a brick-red layer of dust. Only the eyes were still visible. They expressed amazement and fear. Exhausted, hungry, discouraged and angry, they ran back to the rocket to come back to their dear planet Earth as fast as possible!

> **Rappel**
> Il n'y a pas de correspondance de l'idée de passé entre l'anglais et le français. Ainsi, *he went* peut se traduire par « il alla », « il est allé » ou « il allait » suivant le contexte.

13 *Present perfect* ____ p. 25

1 1. applied – 2. have been eating – 3. was looking; saw – 4. was shining – 5. cleaned – 6. have not written – 7. have read; have forgotten – 8. were singing.

2 1. He has not found the ideal flat yet. – 2. He visited six of them last week. – 3. Somebody has been smoking here. Open the window! – 4. He was thinking of her. She was dreaming of him. They finally met last week. – 5. How many cups of coffee have you drunk today?

14 *Past perfect* ____ p. 26

1 arrived – realised – had forgotten – had never happened – grasped – had offered – had asked – tried – remembered – he had not asked – had never felt.

2 1. why he had not answered her letter. – 2. he had already answered her letter. – 3. she had been waiting for it for ages.

3 1. I had already bought my car when I realised it was damaged. – 2. I had been dreaming of this car for years. – 3. My friend had told me it was the best.

15 *Ago, for, since* ____ p. 27

1 1. for – 2. for – 3. ago – 4. since – 5. for – 6. for.

2 1. David Lodge was born eighty-three years ago. – 2. He has been writing novels since 1960. – 3. He taught literature for twenty-seven years. – 4. He has lived in Birmingham for fifty-eight years.

> **Attention**
> *Ago* est uniquement un marqueur de temps. Ne pas confondre avec *there is/there are*.

16 L'expression du futur ____ p. 28

1 1. a – 2. b – 3. c – 4. e – 5. c – 6. b – 7. f – 8. d.

2 1. is going to – 2. will – 3. will – 4. is going to.

3 1. *be about to* → Hurry up! A glass of water, please, he is about to faint! – 2. *be going to* → If you ski off-piste, you are going to start an avalanche. – 3. *will* → It's too hot here. I will open the window. – 4. présent simple → According to the schedule, the plane takes off at 5 p.m.

17 La condition, l'hypothèse ____ p. 29

1 1. c (irréel du présent) – 2. b (conséquence à venir) – 3. d (irréel du passé) – 4. d (irréel du passé).

2 1. had taken – 2. 'll visit – 3. 'd call – 4. stop – 5. invited – 6. wouldn't have gone out.

3 *Corrigé suggéré :* 1. ...I would call the police. – 2. ...I won't trust him anymore. – 3. ...I would be able to pay you back. – 4. If he goes on insulting me...

18 Souhaits et regrets ____ p. 30

1 1. I – 2. R – 3. I – 4. I – 5. R.

2 1. J'aimerais que mon fils travaille mieux. – 2. Si seulement j'avais plus de temps pour étudier. – 3. Je regrette qu'il ait abandonné ses études. – 4. J'aurais mieux fait de demander la santé et l'amour.

> **Remarque**
> Ici, *wish* n'est pas l'équivalent de « je souhaite » en français.
> **Ex. :** *I wish he would work better* (= je voudrais/j'aimerais qu'il travaille mieux) ≠ *I wish you a merry Christmas.*

3 1. I wish you stopped smoking./I wish you to stop smoking. – 2. I wish you could play the piano.

Nouveau
Cahier du jour
Cahier du soir

Mémento visuel
Anglais 3e

À détacher et à conserver toute l'année !

Le comparatif et le superlatif

Comparatif : pour comparer deux éléments entre eux

Supériorité

- Adjectifs longs :
more + adjectif + *than*
*Tom is **more** athletic **than** Drew.*
- Adjectifs courts :
adjectif + *-er* + *than*
*Tom is small**er than** Drew.*

Infériorité

- *Less* + adjectif + *than*
*Tom is **less** tall **than** Drew.*
- *Not as* + adjectif + *as*
*Tom is not **as** tall **as** Drew.*

Égalité

As + adjectif + *as*
*Tom is **as** athletic **as** Drew.*

Superlatif : pour comparer un élément par rapport à tous les autres

Supériorité

- Adjectifs longs : *the most* + adjectif
*Betty is **the most** athletic girl in the class.*
- Adjectifs courts : *the* + adjectif + *-est*
*Betty is **the** short**est** girl in the class.*

Infériorité

The least + adjectif
*Veronica is **the least** polite girl in the class.*

Les adjectifs

Longs

2 syllabes ou plus

Courts

- 1 syllabe
- 2 syllabes se terminant par ***y*** ou ***ow*** (*funny, narrow*)

Exceptions

- good → better – the best
- bad → worse – the worst
- far → further – the furthest
→ farther – the farthest

Le prétérit et le *present perfect*

Le prétérit

- Action passée, datée, terminée
- BV + *-ed* ou verbes irréguliers
- Auxiliaire *did*

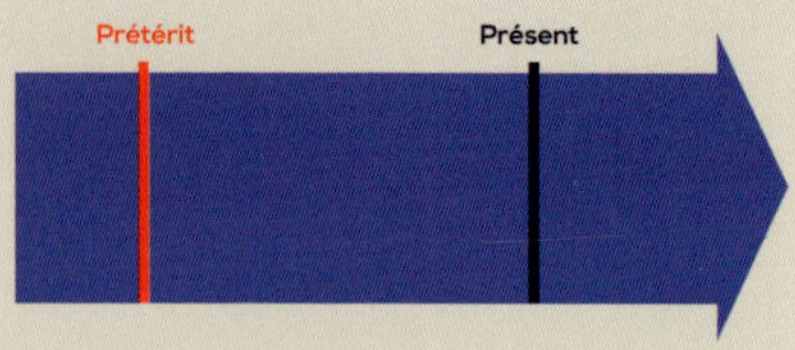

Le *present perfect*

- Action commencée dans le passé et qui est toujours d'actualité ou qui a toujours un impact au moment où l'on parle
- *Have/has* + participe passé
- Participe passé = BV + *-ed* ou verbes irréguliers

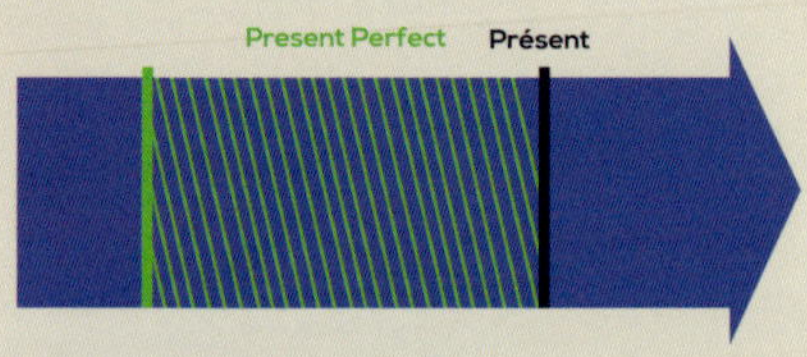

For, since, during, ago

For, since

- Pour dire *depuis*
- *For* + durée

*She has worked at the restaurant **for** 10 years.*

- *Since* + date ou moment précis

*She has lived in Paris **since** 2009.*

For, during

- Pour dire *pendant*

*She worked at the restaurant **for** 10 years.*

*She stayed in her room **during** dinner.*

Ago

- Pour dire *il y a* + durée

*She had lunch two hours **ago**.*

Exprimer ses idées

Les degrés de probabilité

Pensées

- I think/I suppose/ I assume…
- maybe/probably/ perhaps/possibly…
- a thought/an idea/ an opinion…

Sentiments

- I feel
- a feeling/an emotion

sad/scared/ worried

happy/joyful/ glad

Exprimer son accord ou son désaccord

I agree with you.

I disagree with you.

Attention : pas besoin de *be*

Les adverbes d'intensité

Tom is ***so*** *funny!*

This flower is ***really*** *beautiful!*

Mike is ***very*** *tall!*

Les degrés de probabilité

Might

Probabilité faible

Amy is not here, she ***might*** *be sick.*

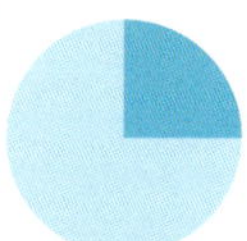

+ 25 %

May

Probabilité moyenne

Amy is not here, she ***may*** *be sick.*

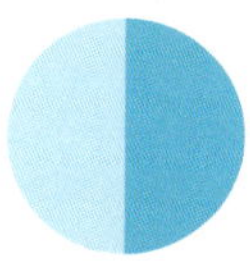

+ 50 %

Must

Probabilité forte

Amy is not here, she ***must*** *be sick.*

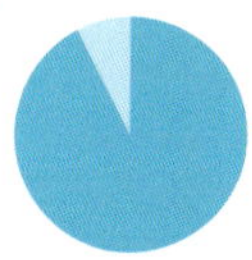

+ 90 %

Les souhaits et les regrets

L'expression du futur

Be going to + BV

- Pour exprimer le futur proche.
- Sujet + *be* au présent simple + *going to* + BV
  *Look at the sky! It **is going to** rain.*
- Forme négative :
  Sujet + *be* + *not* + *going to* + BV
- Forme interrogative :
  Be + sujet + *going to* + BV + ?

Will + BV

- Pour exprimer un futur plus lointain, plus incertain, ou un engagement.

- Sujet + *will* + BV
  *I **will be** 18 next December.*
- Forme négative :
  Sujet + *will not* ou *won't* + BV
- Forme interrogative :
  Will + sujet + BV

Le conditionnel

Would

Pour parler d'une situation qui n'existe que sous certaines conditions.
*If I had a dog, I **would** walk it every day.*

Could

Pour dire ce que l'on pourrait faire (verbe *pouvoir* au conditionnel).
*If I had a dog, I **could** play with it.*

Should

Pour parler de ce qu'on devrait faire, donner un conseil (verbe *devoir* au conditionnel).
*If you have a dog, you **should** walk it every day.*

L'expression du regret

Au présent

- On regrette quelque chose qui se passe au moment où l'on parle.
- *Wish* + prétérit
  *I **wish** I had a big brother.*

Au passé

- On regrette que quelque chose ne se soit pas déroulé comme on l'aurait souhaité dans le passé.
- *Wish* + *had* + participe passé
  *I **wish** you **had** helped me.*

Le désir de changer les choses

- On émet le souhait d'un changement au présent.
- *Wish* + *would* + BV
  I wish you would help me.

19 *Can/can't* p. 31

1 1. impossibilité dans le passé – 2. irréel du passé – 3. impossibilité dans le présent – 4. demande d'autorisation – 5. refus de permission – 6. hypothèse – 7. possibilité.

2 1. You could do it last week. – 2. He can't come. I forbid you. – 3. He could have come during the holidays. – 4. He can't have slept until midday. – 5. She could dance for hours.

20 *May/might* p. 32

1 1. demande de permission – 2. probabilité – 3. reproche – 4. incertitude – 5. irréel du passé – 6. reproche.

2 1. can't – 2. may – 3. may/might.

3 1. He may have lied. – 2. She may have waited too long. – 3. You might have tried a second time. – 4. She may have discovered our secret.

21 *Must/mustn't* p. 33

1 contrainte : 4. et 6. – probabilité dans le présent : 3. – probabilité dans le passé : 1. et 2. – interdiction : 5. – absence d'obligation : 7.

2 1. will have to wear – 2. must have forgotten – 3. must have missed – 4. must be – 5. mustn't ski – 6. had to type.

3 1. There must be a garage in this street. – 2. He must have been kept at his office. – 3. She had to take the bus every morning at 8 o'clock.

22 *Will/would* p. 34

1 1. Young people will always have an outing. – 2. Oh! Yes, I will. – 3. Formerly I would take long walks. – 4. The grandfather wouldn't answer this question. – 5. They said the weather would be fine. – 6. I won't.

> **Attention**
> Ne pas confondre *would*, habitude dans le passé (phrase 3), et *would*, conditionnel (phrase 5).

2 1. wouldn't – 2. will – 3. won't – 4. will.

23 *Shall/should* p. 35

1 1. b. – 2. b. – 3. a. – 4. c. – 5. a.

2 1. Let's go swimming, shall we? – 2. You should have brought your swimsuit. – 3. You should take the plane; it's faster. – 4. People shouldn't drive so fast on motorways.

24 L'infinitif p. 36

1 1. play – 2. me to listen to – 3. attend – 4. is said to be – 5. let me go – 6. to play – 7. buy.

> **Attention**
> Ne pas confondre *I'd rather* (= j'aimerais mieux) et *I'd better* (= je ferais mieux).

2 1. The doctor wants me to eat less. – 2. I'd rather practise sports more often. – 3. Sports make you run and jump. – 4. It is said to be good for health. – 5. Let's go. Why not try immediately? – 6. All parents wish their children to be healthy.

25 Structures en *-ing* (1) p. 37

1 1. I hate working when the weather is fine. – 2. Immediately after reading his/her letter, I started answering him/her. – 3. I remember seeing this play two years ago. – 4. I enjoy going to the theatre very much. – 5. I'm used to reading for ten minutes before going to sleep. – 6. I prefer swimming to skiing.

2 1. see; use – 2. to start looking for – 3. cycling; to drink – 4. having – 5. practising – 6. playing; listening to.

26 Structures en *-ing* (2) p. 38

1 1. Ça lui était égal de faire les vitres toutes les semaines. – 2. Il ne supporte pas la présence des chats à cause de son asthme. – 3. Ça vaut la peine d'acheter cet ordinateur. – 4. Elle ne pouvait s'empêcher de crier quand un but était marqué. – 5. Ça ne me dit rien d'inventer des choses dont les gens ne se serviront pas. – 6. Aider les pauvres ne l'intéresse pas ; il est trop occupé à s'enrichir.

2 *Corrigé suggéré :* 1. It's no use complaining about the weather; you can't help it. – 2. She always enjoyed taking long walks with her grandfather. – 3. My sister is used to ringing up her friends after midnight. – 4. I'd like to visit Morocco in winter. – 5. My grandmother is fond of travelling but her husband hates visiting foreign countries. – 6. A lot of thanks for offering me such a splendid birthday present.

27 Le passif p. 39

1 1. All the newspapers have been sold (by the newsagent). – 2. The actress was sent flowers by a secret admirer. – 3. The play was reported by the journalist to have been a great success. – 4. The preacher was listened to attentively by the audience.

2 1. was organised – 2. had been sent – 3. will be appreciated – 4. shouldn't be fascinated – 5. hasn't been carried away.

28 Les propositions subordonnées p. 40

1 1. shines – 2. comes – 3. am – 4. retire – 5. had – 6. managed.

> **Rappel**
> Pas de forme future après *when*.

2 1. Until – 2. as soon as – 3. although – 4. While.

3 1. Elle se sentit récompensée quand elle eut fini son ouvrage. – 2. Dès qu'on lui offrirait un travail, elle l'accepterait. – 3. Jusqu'à ce qu'elle eût parlé, personne ne s'était aperçu qu'elle était française.

29 Les propositions subordonnées relatives p. 41

1 1. where – 2. which – 3. whose – 4. that – 5. when.

2 1. I didn't like the person I was introduced to. – 2. She visited a museum whose paintings were too modern for her. – 3. All the children who were tired went to bed.

> **Rappel**
> Jamais d'article après *whose*.

3 1. I don't know what you want. – 2. Can you lend me the book (that) I need?

30 Le style indirect p. 42

1 1. "I (have) visited a haunted castle in Scotland." – 2. "Do you believe in ghosts?" – 3. "I'll believe in ghosts when I see one." – 4. "Don't laugh at me."

2 1. if I was all right. – 2. that he flew to New York once a month. – 3. not to ask silly questions. – 4. that he would settle in India the following year.

31 L'article (cas général) p. 43

1 1. Let me tell you a story. **The** story is about Ø dinosaurs. – 2. Ø Dinosaurs have never been Ø faithful friends of Ø men. – 3. Junior said he had seen a dinosaur in **the** park. – 4. **The** dinosaurs I saw in **the** film were frightening. – 5. **The** heroes of **the** film were Ø good actors. – 6. They showed Ø great courage and saved **the** world. – 7. **The** film showed that **the**

prehistoric world was not a paradise. – **8.** **The** special effects in Ø Spielberg's film were a great technical success. – **9.** Ø Professor Smith, a famous archeologist, got excited when he discovered **the** remains of a dinosaur. – **10.** He is going to write **an** article for **the** best-known paper in Ø Great Britain.

2 **1.** The jewels I've bought are shining in the sun. – **2.** Women like jewels. – **3.** Last night I was woken up by a noise. – **4.** The noise came from the dining room downstairs.

32 L'article (cas particuliers) p. 44

1 **the:** **1.** the Johnsons (nom de famille au pluriel) – **2.** the Thames (fleuve) – **3.** the guitar (instrument de musique) – Ø: **4.** Kent (région) – **5.** milk (aliment) – **6.** nature (nom abstrait).

2 **1.** Mr Plunket knocked at **the** door; Ø supper was ready. – **2.** Mrs Plunket was sitting at **the** desk in **the** office, reading **the** papers. – **3.** In this place you go to Ø bed at 8 and don't get **the** football news on TV. – **4.** Ø Queen Elizabeth II was born in Ø Bruton street, in Ø London. – **5.** In **the** morning we would go from **the** City to **the** mouth of **the** Thames.

3 **1.** In the morning he drinks white coffee and eats toasts. – **2.** People are not always keen on doing housework and ironing.

33 Dénombrables et indénombrables p. 45

1 **1.** noise – **5.** ham – **7.** traffic jam – **8.** currency.

2 **3.** job – **5.** time – **7.** experience – **8.** forget-me-not – **10.** room.

3 **1.** His/her luggage was delivered at the hotel yesterday. – **2.** Modern furniture is appreciated by practical people. – **3.** A good piece of information is better than a good piece of advice. – **4.** People listen to the news every morning. – **5.** The police have noticed that the goods were damaged.

34 Les quantificateurs p. 46

1 **1.** a lot of; much – **2.** how many; a few – **3.** much; little.

2 **1.** some – **2.** no; any – **3.** something; nobody – **4.** nowhere; anywhere – **5.** anybody; some – **6.** no; no; nothing.

3 **1.** I have a lot of luck but I don't have much money. – **2.** A few people say that they never have enough of it.

35 Comparatif et superlatif p. 47

1 **1.** Everest is more dangerous to climb than Mont Blanc. – **2.** The Empire State Building is higher than the Eiffel Tower. – **3.** Everest is the highest mountain in the world. – **4.** Warsaw is the least expensive city in Europe.

2 **1.** It is more and more difficult to find a flat. – **2.** Traffic is worse in Mexico City than in Paris.

36 Accord et désaccord ; similitude et contraste p. 48

1 **1. a.** Neither has Peter; **b.** Peter has. – **2. a.** So is her brother; **b.** Her brother is not. – **3. a.** So should her sister; **b.** Her sister shouldn't. – **4. a.** Neither did her parents ; **b.** Her parents did.

2 **1.** Mary was attending a wedding while her husband was attending a football match. – **2.** Mary is very good at maths whereas Peter is good at sports. – **3.** Cléante likes spending money whereas Harpagon wants to keep it. – **4.** My father was still at work while my mother was already on holiday.

37 Le génitif p. 49

1 **1.** my parents' car – **2.** the children's bicycles – **3.** the Johnsons' computer – **4.** a one hour's walk – **5.** my uncle's (house).

2 **1.** Don't touch your sister's computer; it is not a children's toy (pluriel nécessaire en anglais). – **2.** I'll go to Mark's party with a friend of Mary's. – **3.** My mother goes to the hairdresser's every week. – **4.** As I don't have a smartphone, I borrow my father's.

38 L'exclamation p. 50

1 **1.** such a – **2.** so – **3.** such – **4.** such.

2 **1. a.** How clever this boy is! – **b.** He is such a clever boy! – **2. a.** This man looks so miserable!; **b.** How miserable this man looks! – **3. a.** What wonderful years I've spent abroad!; **b.** I've spent such wonderful years abroad! – **4. a.** What awful weather today!; **b.** How awful the weather is today!

3 **1.** What a splendid carpet! I've never seen such beautiful colours! – **2.** What talent! There is so much love in his/her paintings! – **3.** What a discovery! But Christopher Columbus was such a good sailor!

Corrigés détachables

19 Can/can't

→ Corrigés p. III

Observer et retenir

Can I or can't I?

JOURNALIST – **Can** you do it? I'm sure you **can't**.

RAMBO – **Can** I have a try?

JOURNALIST – Of course, you **can**.

RAMBO – Look! Here you are. I **can** do it.

JOURNALIST – I didn't think you **could do** it. I **couldn't** imagine you **could have done** it.

RAMBO – I **could do** it as many times as you want.

SUPERMAN – You cheated. You **can't have done** it.

■ *Can* exprime :

- une capacité physique ou intellectuelle

Ex. : *Can you do it?*

- une demande de permission

Ex. : *Can I have a try?*

■ *Can't* exprime :

- une incapacité physique ou intellectuelle

Ex. : *I'm sure you can't.*

- un refus de permission

Ex. : *No, you can't have another try.*

■ *Can't + have +* participe passé exprime l'impossibilité, à valeur de bilan.

Ex. : *You can't have done it.*

■ *Could* exprime :

- les mêmes valeurs que *can*, au passé
- l'hypothèse

Ex. : *I could do it as many times as you want.*

■ *Could + have +* participe passé exprime l'irréel du passé.

Ex. : *You could have done it if you had wanted to.*

■ *Couldn't* exprime les mêmes valeurs que ***can't*** au passé.

Ex. : *He couldn't have forgotten his name.*

■ *Couldn't + have +* participe passé exprime l'impossibilité dans le passé.

Ex. : *As he was in hospital, he couldn't have killed this man.*

Remarque

Be able to remplace *can* au *present perfect*, au *past perfect*, à l'infinitif et au futur.

S'entraîner

1 ★★ Indiquez, pour chaque phrase, la valeur du modal.

1. I went to the cinema with Mary. – You can't have done that! ....
2. You could have worked a little longer. ....
3. I can't do more; I'm exhausted. ....
4. Can I go swimming? ....
5. No, you can't. ....
6. Couldn't you be a little more serious? ....
7. I'm sure you can work better. ....

2 ★★★ Traduisez les phrases suivantes.

1. Tu savais le faire la semaine dernière. ....
2. Il est impossible qu'il vienne. Je te l'interdis. ....
3. Il aurait pu venir pendant les vacances. ....
4. Il est impossible qu'il ait dormi jusqu'à midi. ....
5. Elle pourrait danser pendant des heures. ....

Auto évaluation Très bien ☐ Bien ☐ Pas assez bien ☐

20 May/might

→ Corrigés p. III

Observer et retenir

Hypotheses

SON – Peter's late. I'm worried. He **may have had** an accident.

FATHER – No, John. He **might** still **be playing** his match. You **might** go and meet him. By the way, **he might have phoned**.

SON – Anyway, **may I go** now?

FATHER – Yes, you can. Better take your umbrella. It **might rain**.

■ ***May*** exprime :
– la demande de permission (**ex. :** *May I go now?*) ;
– la probabilité (**ex. :** *He may have forgotten our appointment*).

■ ***May + have* + participe passé** exprime une supposition (évènement passé).
Ex. : *He may have had an accident.*

■ ***Might*** exprime :
– une probabilité plus faible (**ex. :** *It might rain*) ;
– une suggestion (**ex. :** *You might go and meet him*).

■ ***Might + have* + participe passé** exprime :
– un irréel du passé (**ex. :** *He might have had an accident*) ;
– un reproche (**ex. :** *He might have phoned*).

Remarque
Be allowed to remplace ***may/might*** au *present perfect*, au *past perfect*, à l'infinitif et pour indiquer une nuance de futur, avec le sens de **être autorisé à**.

S'entraîner

1 ★ Cochez les valeurs du modal dans les phrases suivantes.

1. May I leave my suitcase here? ☐ probabilité ☐ demande de permission
2. He may not be ready on time. ☐ reproche ☐ probabilité
3. He might have packed sooner. ☐ reproche ☐ suggestion
4. It might be OK after all. ☐ incertitude ☐ suggestion
5. It was too risky. She might have broken her leg. ☐ reproche ☐ irréel du passé
6. You are not serious. You might have told me. ☐ reproche ☐ irréel du passé

2 ★★ Complétez les phrases suivantes avec *can* ou *may* au présent ou au passé.

1. I .... climb up Mount Everest; it's too high for me.
2. You .... have got your driving licence but you don't drive properly.
3. She is cross. She .... have thought we were jealous.

3 ★★★ Sur une feuille à part, traduisez les phrases suivantes.

1. Il se peut qu'il ait menti.
2. Elle a peut-être attendu trop longtemps.
3. Vous auriez pu essayer une deuxième fois.
4. Elle a pu deviner notre secret.

Auto évaluation Très bien ☐ Bien ☐ Pas assez bien ☐

21 Must/mustn't

→ Corrigés p. III

Observer et retenir

A new job

SARAH – What about Lucy? Always on the dole? She **must have acquired** (1) a lot of experience in her previous job. She **must have found** (2) a job by now.

VICKI – Yes, she has. I'm very glad for her.

SARAH – It **must be hard** (3) for her to work again. She has been unemployed for so long.

VICKI – Certainly. The more so as she **must** always **arrive** (4) on time, she **mustn't smoke** (5) in her office. And the manager told her that she **must** always **finish** (6) her work before leaving.

SARAH – I hope she **doesn't have to work** (7) at weekends.

■ ***Must*** exprime :

– une contrainte (**ex. :** *He must work hard to succeed*) ;

– une forte probabilité (**ex. :** *It's 4. He must be on the train*).

■ ***Mustn't*** exprime une interdiction.

Exemple *You mustn't speak in a church.*

■ ***Must + have + participe passé*** exprime :

– une contrainte (**ex. :** *You must have finished your work tonight or you'll be punished*) ;

– une forte probabilité (**ex. :** *You must have read this book before to be able to talk about it so easily*).

■ Au *past simple*, au *present perfect*, au *past perfect* et pour rendre un aspect du futur, on utilise ***have to***.

Exemple *You'll have to be more attentive.*

Rappel

Une contrainte « extérieure » s'exprime par ***have to***.

→ *I have to go now. I've got an appointment.*

Attention

L'absence d'obligation se rend par ***don't have to***.

→ *You don't have to bring your skis; you can rent them in a shop.*

Attention

Dans le discours indirect, on utilise généralement ***must*** au passé (la forme reste la même).

→ *The teacher said that we must visit this museum.*

S'entraîner

1 ★ Repérez les différentes valeurs des formes verbales en gras dans le dialogue ci-dessus (chiffres 1 à 7). Écrivez ces chiffres dans le tableau.

contrainte	
probabilité dans le présent	
probabilité dans le passé	
interdiction	
absence d'obligation	

2 ★★ Complétez les phrases suivantes avec *must* ou *have to* à la forme et à l'aspect voulus. Utilisez les verbes indiqués entre parenthèses.

1. If you enter this school, you .... a uniform. *(wear)*
2. It's all lit up; the old lady .... to switch off the light. *(forget)*
3. My friend is not here yet. He .... his train. *(miss)*
4. She passed her exam with honours. She .... bright. *(be)*
5. It's strictly forbidden. You .... here. *(ski)*
6. When she was at school, she .... her papers on a computer. *(type)*

3 ★★★ Traduisez sur une feuille à part.

1. Il doit y avoir un garage dans cette rue.
2. Il a dû être retenu à son bureau.
3. Elle devait prendre le bus tous les matins à 8 heures.

Auto évaluation Très bien ☐ Bien ☐ Pas assez bien ☐

22 Will/would

→ Corrigés p. III

Observer et retenir

Taking a walk or not

GRANDDAUGHTER – On the radio they said the weather **would be** fine. I'm sure it**'ll be** fine. **Will you come** to the park with me?

GRANDMOTHER – Oh, yes. **I will**.

GRANDFATHER – **I won't**; it's too far. Young people **will always have** an outing when the sun shines.

GRANDDAUGHTER – Are you so exhausted?

[THE GRANDFATHER **wouldn't answer** this question]

GRANDFATHER – Formerly, I **would take** long walks in the forest but now… Goodbye. And shut the door silently, **will you?**

■ ***Will*** exprime :
- une **décision immédiate** (**ex. :** *Don't move, I'll answer the phone*) ;
- une **prédiction** (**ex. :** *The weather will be fine*) ;
- la **volonté** (**ex. :** *I will stop smoking*) ;
- le **refus**, à la forme négative (**ex. :** *I won't go to the park*) ;
- une **caractéristique immuable** (**ex. :** *He is very pious; he will go to church every day*) ;
- une **demande polie**, à la forme interrogative (**ex. :** *Will you open the window, please?*).

■ ***Would*** exprime :
- une **prédiction** dans le passé (**ex. :** *He told me the weather would be fine*) ;
- la **volonté** dans le passé (**ex. :** *He would do it, but he couldn't*) ;
- le **refus** dans le passé à la forme négative (**ex. :** *He wouldn't answer*) ;
- une **habitude passée** (**ex. :** *In the past he would go to church every day*) ;
- une **demande très polie** à la forme interrogative (**ex. :** *Would you open the door, please?*).

S'entraîner

1 ★★ Trouvez, dans le dialogue ci-dessus, les phrases dans lesquelles *will* et *would* ont la même valeur que dans les phrases ci-dessous et écrivez-les.

1. Boys will be boys.

....

....

2. Will you marry me?

....

....

3. When he was young, he would dance every Saturday night.

....

....

4. His mother asked him to do it but he wouldn't.

....

....

5. She exclaimed she would get furious against him.

....

....

6. Try and tell her, but I'm sure she won't accept.

....

....

2 ★★★ Complétez les phrases suivantes avec *will*, *won't*, *would* ou *wouldn't* suivant le sens.

1. She .... marry him because she hated him.
2. If you marry me you .... be happy.
3. I .... say anything; it's a secret.
4. There .... be more and more cybernauts on the Web.

Auto évaluation Très bien ☐ Bien ☐ Pas assez bien ☐

23 Shall/should

→ Corrigés p. III

Observer et retenir

Entertainment or work

JACK – I've something to suggest. **Shall** we **go** to the cinema?

JIM – I can't. I've too much work.

JACK – Not so much! It's 11 o'clock. You **should have finished** by now.

JIM – But it's longer than I thought it **would** be.

JACK – If so, you **should have phoned** me yesterday. Anyway, you **shouldn't work** so much. You **should enjoy** seeing films. Let's go to the cinema, **shall** we? What time **shall we meet** there?

■ ***Shall*** s'emploie à la 1re personne pour exprimer :

– une **suggestion** (**ex. :** *Shall we go to the cinema?*) ;

– une **reprise** en fin de phrase, après un impératif ; on emploie alors la 1re personne du pluriel (**ex. :** *Let's go to the cinema, shall we?*).

■ ***Should*** s'emploie à toutes les personnes pour exprimer :

– un **conseil**, à la forme affirmative (**ex. :** *You should practise sport more often*) ;

– un **reproche**, à la forme négative (**ex. :** *You shouldn't smoke so much*) ;

– la **probabilité** (**ex. :** *If you hurry, you should be there on time*).

■ ***Should*** + ***have*** + **participe passé** exprime :

– un **bilan** (**ex. :** *You should have finished at 11; it's so easy*) ;

– un **reproche** ou un **regret** (**ex. :** *You should have started earlier; now you're late*).

Remarque

Pour exprimer le **conseil**, on emploie aussi ***'d better* (*had better*)**.

→ *You'd better take a rest.*

(Tu ferais mieux de te reposer.)

S'entraîner

1 ★ Cochez la case qui correspond à la valeur des modaux.

1. Shall we organise a party next Saturday?	☐ **a.** ordre	☐ **b.** proposition	☐ **c.** reproche
2. He should be more careful when crossing the street.	☐ **a.** regret	☐ **b.** critique	☐ **c.** suggestion
3. The board should have elected another president.	☐ **a.** reproche	☐ **b.** suggestion	☐ **c.** probabilité
4. I shouldn't have been so rude. Now he is vexed.	☐ **a.** promesse	☐ **b.** obligation	☐ **c.** regret
5. It's Monday. He should be at work.	☐ **a.** probabilité	☐ **b.** regret	☐ **c.** ordre

2 ★★ Reformulez les phrases suivantes en utilisant *shall*, *should*, *shouldn't* ou *shouldn't have + -ed*.

1. Why not go swimming? ....

2. I wish you had brought your swimsuit. ....

3. You'd better take the plane: it's faster. ....

4. It is dangerous for people to drive so fast on motorways. ....

Auto évaluation Très bien ☐ Bien ☐ Pas assez bien ☐

24 L'infinitif

→ Corrigés p. III

Observer et retenir

Learning languages

I'd **like to study** Chinese but I **can hear** my parents say: "We **want you to speak** English fluently first." They have bought many English books **for me to read** but I'**d rather go** to the States **to meet** Americans. **It is said to be** the best way **to learn** English. It **makes** you **talk** more easily. I hope they'll **let me go** over there. If I **want them to accept**, I'**d better be** serious!

■ ***To* + base verbale** indique une visée.

Cette forme s'utilise :

– après les verbes de **volonté**, de **souhait**, d'**ordre** (**ex. :** *I'd like to visit the USA. I want you to visit the USA*) ;

– après un **passif** (**ex. :** *He was said to be a good doctor*) ;

– pour indiquer un **but** (**ex. :** *I need this grammar to learn English. I bought this grammar for you to learn English*).

■ La **base verbale seule** s'utilise :

– après ***let*** et les **modaux** (**ex. :** *Let's go... I can hear...*) ;

– après les verbes de **perception** (**ex. :** *I can hear them say...*) ;

– après ***make***, au sens de « faire faire » (**ex. :** *This teacher made me work hard*) ;

– après ***why***, qui est un interrogatif de suggestion (**ex. :** *Why not visit this museum?*) ;

– après ***I'd better***, ***I'd rather*** (**ex. :** *I'd rather go to the zoo but I'd better stay at home to work*).

S'entraîner

1 ★ Complétez les phrases avec *to* + base verbale ou une base verbale seule. Utilisez le verbe indiqué entre parenthèses.

1. The conductor makes his musicians .... in tune. *(play)*

2. My parents want .... classical music. *(me/listen to)*

3. I'd rather .... a techno music concert. *(attend)*

4. This musical group .... excellent. *(say/be)*

Conseil
Utilisez un passif.

5. They won't .... me .... to the Zenith. *(let/go)*

6. I'd like .... an instrument. *(play)*

7. You'd better .... CD's. *(buy)*

2 ★★ Traduisez les phrases suivantes.

1. Le docteur veut que je mange moins.

....

2. J'aimerais mieux faire du sport plus souvent.

....

3. Les sports vous font courir et sauter.

....

4. On dit que c'est bon pour la santé.

....

5. Allons-y ! Pourquoi ne pas essayer immédiatement ?

....

6. Tous les parents souhaitent que leurs enfants soient en bonne santé.

....

Auto évaluation — Très bien ☐ Bien ☐ Pas assez bien ☐

25 Structures en *-ing* (1)

→ Corrigés p. III

Observer et retenir

Interviewing a postman

"Before **starting** a busy day, I like **having** a good breakfast... **Delivering** letters is a pleasant job... I meet a lot of people and enjoy **talking** with them... I'm never tired of **walking** since at weekends I'm used to **going jogging**!... I remember **meeting** an old lady..." And he went on **telling** stories; he could not stop **talking**.

Fonction nominale (sujet ou complément)

Exemple *Jogging is a healthy activity. He practised jogging when he was younger.*

Fonction « gérondif »

- après les **verbes d'appréciation**

Exemple *I like jogging.*

- après les verbes indiquant un **début**, une **continuité** ou une **fin** d'action

Exemple *I started jogging at ten. He kept speaking for hours.*

- après des **prépositions**

Exemple *Before jogging, he has a good breakfast.*

- après certains verbes tels que : ***avoid***, ***remember***, ***suggest*** dans certains cas

Exemple *He remembers visiting the Empire State Building a long time ago.*

Attention
Il existe deux cas où **to** est suivi d'un gérondif.
→ *I'm **looking forward to** hearing from you.*
→ *I'm **used to** jogging every morning.*

S'entraîner

1 ★★ **Traduisez les phrases suivantes.**

1. Je déteste travailler quand il fait beau.

....

2. Immédiatement après avoir lu sa lettre, j'ai commencé à lui répondre.

....

3. Je me rappelle avoir vu cette pièce il y a deux ans.

....

4. J'aime beaucoup aller au théâtre.

....

Conseil
Utilisez *enjoy*.

5. J'ai l'habitude de lire pendant dix minutes avant de m'endormir.

....

6. Je préfère la natation au ski.

....

2 ★★ **Complétez les phrases suivantes avec une base verbale, *to* + base verbale ou une structure en *-ing*. Utilisez les verbes donnés entre parenthèses.**

1. I'd rather .... you than .... a computer. *(see/use)*
2. He has been told .... another job. *(start/look for)*
3. He stopped .... for a moment .... a beer. *(cycle/drink)*
4. She remembers .... tea with me on a Saturday afternoon. *(have)*
5. He gave up .... sport after his accident. *(practise)*
6. .... an instrument is certainly more rewarding than just .... music on the radio. *(play/listen to)*

Auto évaluation — Très bien ☐ Bien ☐ Pas assez bien ☐

26 Structures en *-ing* (2)

→ Corrigés p. III

Observer et retenir

Are proverbs true?

FIONA – Let me apologise for **breaking** this plate. I'm sorry.
PHYLLIS – It's no use **crying** over spilt milk.
FIONA – You're right. But I can't help **apologising**.
PHYLLIS – By the way, are you fond of **using** proverbs?
FIONA – Some of them are worth **learning**. But I don't feel like **using** them all the time.
PHYLLIS – Anyway, thanks for **coming**. It was nice **having** you here.

■ Un certain nombre d'**expressions** sont **suivies d'un verbe en *-ing***.

■ Elles peuvent être formées :
- à base de verbes : apologise (***for***), excuse (***for***), ***feel like, I can't bear, I can't help, I don't mind***…

Exemple *I can't help apologising.*

- à base de noms : ***thanks for, it's no use***…

Exemple *It's no use crying over spilt milk.*

- à base d'adjectifs : ***be busy, be interested in, it's worth***…

Exemple *This book is worth reading.*

Cas particuliers
- ***nice*** + évènement **présent**
→ *nice to meet you.*
- ***nice*** + évènement **passé**
→ *it was nice having…*
- ***no*** (interdiction officielle)
→ *No smoking.*

S'entraîner

1 ★★ **Traduisez les phrases suivantes.**

1. She didn't mind cleaning the panes every week.

....

2. He can't bear having cats around him because of his asthma.

....

3. This computer is worth buying.

....

4. She couldn't help shouting when a goal was scored.

....

5. I don't feel like inventing things people will never use.

....

6. He is not interested in helping the poor; he is too busy making money.

....

2 ★★★ **Après avoir relu les fiches 24, 25 et 26, inventez des phrases en utilisant les mots ou expressions indiqués.**

1. it's no use → ....

2. enjoy → ....

3. be used to → ....

4. 'd like → ....

5. hate → ....

6. thanks for → ....

Auto évaluation — Très bien ☐ Bien ☐ Pas assez bien ☐

27 Le passif

→ Corrigés p. III

Observer et retenir

Will the President recover?

The President **is said** to be ill. His private doctor **was sent for**. The President **was ordered** to stay in bed for a week at least. He **was told** not to go abroad. All his appointments **have been cancelled**. A medical bulletin **will be published** tonight. After this week's rest it **is expected** that the President will resume work. *The Liberty Clarion*

Cas général

Sujet + (modal) + ***be*** (conjugué) + verbe au participe passé + (***by*** + complément d'agent)

His appointments *have been* *cancelled* *(by his secretary).*

- Le passif **met en valeur le sujet** de la phrase et ce qui lui arrive.

Cas particuliers

- Avec les verbes à **deux compléments** (*give, show, tell*...), il y a deux constructions possibles :
  - *The baby was given a lovely toy* → On s'intéresse à l'enfant.
  - *A lovely toy was given to the baby* → On s'intéresse au cadeau.
- Avec les verbes **prépositionnels**, on retrouve au passif le groupe verbal suivi de la préposition.

Exemple *Some old people are looked after by nurses.*

- Avec les verbes d'**opinion** (*say, think, expect*...), il y a deux constructions possibles :
  - *The President is said to be ill* → *construction personnelle*
  - *It is said that the President is ill* → *construction impersonnelle*

Remarque

Dans ces deux exemples, le français utilise l'impersonnel ***on***.

→ *On dit que le président est malade.*

S'entraîner

1 ★ Transformez les phrases suivantes à la voix passive.

1. The newsagent has sold all the newspapers.

....

2. A secret admirer sent flowers to the actress.

....

3. The journalist reported that the play had been a great success.

....

....

4. The audience listened to the preacher attentively.

....

....

2 ★★ Complétez les phrases suivantes avec un groupe verbal à la voix passive en utilisant le verbe entre parenthèses au temps/aspect indiqué.

1. An interview .... by his impresario. *(organise/simple past)*
2. He .... letters several times before. *(send/pluperfect)*
3. I'm sure his help .... *(appreciate/future)*
4. But he .... by money. *(fascinate/reproach)*
5. Up to now he .... by ambition. *(not carry away/present perfect)*

Auto évaluation Très bien ☐ Bien ☐ Pas assez bien ☐

28 Les propositions subordonnées

→ Corrigés p. III

Observer et retenir

A new country

As soon as I've got enough money, I'll fly to India. **When I arrive** there, I'll walk through the country **until I find** a place to sleep. Although I like comfort, I want to live with the villagers because, **when I come back** to Britain, I'll have to write a report about life in Indian villages.

P.J. Smith, globe-trotter

Pour les subordonnées :

- nominales en *-ing* → voir fiche 25 ;
- adverbiales en *to* → voir fiche 24 ;
- circonstancielles exprimant la **condition** → voir fiche 17 ;
- de contraste → voir fiche 36.

Français	Anglais
présent	présent simple
imparfait	*past*
futur	présent simple
futur antérieur	*present perfect*
conditionnel présent	*simple past*
conditionnel passé	*pluperfect*

Les subordonnées de :

- cause sont introduites par ***because*** ;
- concession sont introduites par ***although*** ou ***though***

Exemple *Although I like comfort...* ;

- temps sont introduites par ***when, as, as soon as, until***... et sont toujours suivies d'un présent simple

Exemple *As soon as I've got money, I'll fly... ; When I come back to France, I'll have to...*

S'entraîner

1 ★ Dans les phrases suivantes, traduisez seulement la forme verbale soulignée en utilisant le verbe indiqué.

1. Quand le soleil brille, les oiseaux chantent. *(shine)*

....

2. Quand viendra l'hiver, ils se tairont. *(come)*

....

3. Je passerai mon permis dès que j'aurai 18 ans. *(be)*

....

4. Je me reposerai quand je serai à la retraite. *(retire)*

....

5. Si elle avait ce travail, elle voyagerait beaucoup. *(have)* ....

6. Quand son père dirigeait l'usine, il y avait des bénéfices. *(manage)* ....

....

2 ★★ Complétez avec l'une des conjonctions suivantes : ***although*** – ***as soon as*** – ***because*** – ***when*** – ***while*** – ***until***.

1. .... he is twenty, I won't let him drive.
2. She phoned me .... she was ready.
3. I went to the cinema with Mary .... I hate horror films. Aren't I nice?
4. .... I was waiting for her, she was having tea with friends.

3 ★★★ Traduisez.

1. She felt rewarded when she had finished her work.

....

2. As soon as she was offered a job, she would accept it.

....

3. Until she spoke, nobody realised she was French.

....

Auto évaluation Très bien ☐ Bien ☐ Pas assez bien ☐

29 Les propositions subordonnées relatives

→ Corrigés p. III

Observer et retenir

A thank you letter

It was just the time **when** I needed a gift. The vase you've offered me is exactly **what** I wanted. This vase reminds me of a vase **which** was at home and **whose** patterns were nearly the same. This is the best china **that** I've ever seen. My mother, **who** was an artist, used to arrange roses in it, **which** was beautiful. This is the reason **why** I'm so pleased with your present. Guess the place **where** I put it? On my desk, just in front of me, of course…

■ Deux sortes de propositions relatives :

- les **déterminatives** (sans elles, le sens n'est pas complet)

Exemple *The man that I saw yesterday offered me a job.*

- les **appositives** (sans elles, le sens demeure) ; elles sont encadrées par des virgules

Exemple *The manager, who seems very competent, offered me a job.*

Fonction	Personne	Chose/idée
sujet	*who (that)*	*which (that)*
objet	*that*	*which (that)*
génitif	*whose*	*whose*
lieu	–	*where*
temps	–	*when*
raison	–	*why*

■ Préposition + pronom relatif : la préposition est rejetée en fin de relative.

Exemple *It was a job (that) I wasn't looking for.*

- ***What*** (ce qui, ce que) → *What I mean is…*
- ***Which*** (ce qui, ce que) reprend une proposition.

Exemple *He offered me a job, which was unexpected.*

Remarque

That peut s'omettre lorsqu'il est COD. Après un superlatif et après *all, first, last, only,* on emploie ***that*** et non ***which***.

S'entraîner

1 ★ Cochez le pronom relatif qui convient pour chaque phrase.

1. Show me the church .... there is a beautiful clock. ☐ which ☐ where ☐ that
2. The church, ... was built in the 30's, looks like a bunker. ☐ which ☐ who ☐ where
3. A poor man, ... clothes are torn, begs at the church door. ☐ whose ☐ that ☐ who
4. The last man .... had given him a coin looked still poorer. ☐ which ☐ who ☐ that
5. It was a time .... people were not charitable. ☐ which ☐ that ☐ when

2 ★★ Reformulez les énoncés suivants en utilisant une proposition relative.

1. I didn't like this person. I was introduced to her. ....
2. She visited a museum. Its paintings were too modern for her. ....
3. All the children went to bed. They were tired. ....

3 ★★★ Traduisez les phrases suivantes.

1. Je ne sais pas ce que tu veux. ....
2. Peux-tu me prêter le livre dont j'ai besoin ? ....

Auto évaluation — Très bien ☐ Bien ☐ Pas assez bien ☐

30 Le style indirect

→ Corrigés p. III

Observer et retenir

About grandfather

What grandfather said ten years ago.

He said he **had** never **been** better.
He said that he **had visited** London two years **before**.

What grandfather dreams of.

He says that he **would travel** more.
He says that he **would like** to go to the moon.

What grandfather says today.

He says he **has** never **been** ill.
He says that he **has** never **felt** better… and he tells us **to enjoy** life.

Temps et aspects

style direct	style indirect
présent simple	présent simple
past	past/past perfect
present perfect	past perfect
will	would
imperative	to + *base verbale*

Exemples

He told me Susie arrived on Monday.

He told me he had fallen in love with Susie.

Remarque
Si la question est une *yes/no* question, utilisez *if* :
He asked me if I could help him.

Adverbes

style direct	style indirect
yesterday	the day before
tomorrow	the day after
now	then
here	there

Cas de *must*

- obligation immédiate : *had to* (**ex. :** *She said she had to phone him*) ;
- généralité : *must* (**ex. :** *My parents used to say that children must obey their parents*).

S'entraîner

1 ★★ Transformez les phrases suivantes au style direct.

1. He told me he had visited a haunted castle in Scotland.

He told me: ……………………………………………………

……………………………………………………………………

2. His children asked him if he believed in ghosts.

His children asked him: ……………………………………

……………………………………………………………………

3. He answered that he would believe in ghosts when he saw one.

He answered: ………………………………………………

……………………………………………………………………

4. He told his children not to laugh at him.

He told his children: ………………………………………

2 ★★ Transformez les phrases suivantes au style indirect.

1. Are you all right?

He asked me ……………………………………………………

……………………………………………………………………

2. I fly to New York once a month.

He told me ……………………………………………………

……………………………………………………………………

3. Don't ask silly questions!

He told me ……………………………………………………

……………………………………………………………………

4. He'll settle in India next year.

He informed me ………………………………………………

……………………………………………………………………

Auto évaluation — Très bien ☐ Bien ☐ Pas assez bien ☐

31 L'article (cas général)

→ Corrigés p. III

Observer et retenir

Oliver Twist

The story of Ø Oliver Twist is particularly sad. He was **an** orphan. As **a** child living in **the** streets of Ø London he met **a** burglar, Fagin. **The** burglar taught him how to steal Ø money and Ø watches. So he became **a** pickpocket, who stole Ø passers-by's properties without making **a** noise… Fortunately, **some** years later, he turned out to be **a** real gentleman.

Article indéfini

Noms communs :

- concrets au singulier → *a, an*
- concrets au pluriel → *1, 2, 3… some, Ø*
- abstraits indénombrables → *Ø*

L'indéfini s'emploie **toujours** devant un nom concret singulier.

Exemples

*Mr Smith is **a** teacher.*
*Mr Smith, **an** English teacher, …*
*Don't go out without **an** umbrella.*

Article défini

Noms communs :

- dénombrables au singulier → *the*
- dénombrables au pluriel → *Ø*
- indénombrables → *Ø*
- uniques → *the*

Tout nom peut être déterminé par :

– un complément en *of* → ***the** Queen of England*
– une proposition → ***the** man I saw…*
– le contexte → *I've bought a computer and **the** computer doesn't work.*

S'entraîner

1 ★★ **Complétez les phrases suivantes avec : *a* – *an* – *some* – *the* ou *Ø*.**

1. Let me tell you .... story. .... story is about .... dinosaurs.
2. .... dinosaurs have never been .... faithful friends of .... men.
3. Junior said he had seen .... dinosaur in .... park. Isn't he stupid?
4. .... dinosaurs I saw in .... film were frightening.
5. .... heroes of .... film were .... good actors.
6. They showed .... great courage and saved .... world.
7. .... film showed that .... prehistoric world was not .... paradise.
8. .... special effects in .... Spielberg's film were .... great technical success.
9. .... professor Smith, ... famous archeologist, got excited when he discovered .... remains of .... dinosaur.
10. He is going to write .... article for .... best-known paper in .... Great Britain.

2 ★★★ **Traduisez les phrases suivantes.**

1. Les bijoux que j'ai achetés brillent au soleil.

....

2. Les femmes aiment les bijoux.

....

3. La nuit dernière, j'ai été réveillée par un bruit.

....

4. Le bruit venait de la salle à manger au rez-de-chaussée.

....

Auto évaluation Très bien ☐ Bien ☐ Pas assez bien ☐

32 L'article (cas particuliers)

→ Corrigés p. IV

Observer et retenir

The joys of the country

The Johnsons like going to **the** country. Mr Johnson enjoys fishing in **the** sun, in Ø Kent or on **the** banks of **the** Thames. Mrs Johnson is fond of painting Ø nature, of mixing Ø colours, especially Ø blue and Ø yellow. Patrick Johnson prefers playing Ø rugby… or **the** guitar. For him, Ø lunch is **the** best moment of **the** day: drinking Ø milk and eating Ø cherries is ideal to his mind. It's Ø Sunday and Ø spring. Like all **the** British, **the** Johnson family feels happy far from Ø town and Ø school.

■ *The*

– personnes au pluriel : *The Johnsons*
– personnes ou choses considérées comme uniques : *the sun, the Queen*
– mers, rivières, chaînes de montagnes : *the Channel, the Thames, the Rockies*
– pays (au pluriel) : *the USA*
– instruments : *the guitar*
– adjectifs pris comme des noms à sens pluriel : *The British think that not enough is done for the homeless.*

■ Ø (absence d'article)

– personnes au singulier : *Patrick Johnson*
– noms abstraits : *life, nature*
– lieux au singulier : *Britain, Hyde Park*
– aliments et repas : *milk, breakfast*
– matières et matériaux : *cotton*
– jeux et sports : *chess, rugby*
– matières scolaires : *geography, Greek*
– couleurs : *blue and yellow make green*
– jours, mois, saisons : *Wednesday*

S'entraîner

1 ★ Relisez le texte en haut de cette page : relevez 3 mots précédés de l'article défini (*the*) et 3 mots précédés d'aucun article (Ø) et écrivez à quelle catégorie ces mots appartiennent.

the		catégorie	Ø		catégorie
1.	→	....	4.	→	....
2.	→	....	5.	→	....
3.	→	....	6.	→	....

2 ★★ Complétez les phrases suivantes avec *the* ou Ø.

1. Mr Plunket knocked at .... door; .... supper was ready. **2.** Mrs Plunket was sitting at .... desk in .... office reading .... papers. **3.** In this place you go to .... bed at 8 and don't get .... football news on TV. **4.** .... Queen Elizabeth II was born in .... Bruton Street, in .... London. **5.** In .... morning we would go from .... City to .... mouth of .... Thames.

3 ★★★ Traduisez les phrases suivantes.

1. Le matin, il boit du café au lait et mange des toasts. ....

2. Les gens n'aiment pas toujours le ménage et le repassage. ....

Auto évaluation Très bien ☐ Bien ☐ Pas assez bien ☐

33 Dénombrables et indénombrables

→ Corrigés p. IV

Observer et retenir

Panic

PASSENGER 1 – Excuse me. I need **a piece of information**. My **luggage** is lost. My **money** is lost… Where shall I go?

PASSENGER 2 – What's in your luggage?

PASSENGER 1 – That's none of your business. Two **pairs of pyjamas**, my **glasses**…

PASSENGER 2 – If I were you, I'd go to the information desk.

PASSENGER 1 – Thank you for this **piece of advice**. But the best **means** is to call the police. Look! The **police** are coming. I'll ask them.

À savoir
Pour parler d'un élément de l'ensemble, on utilise, suivant le cas : *a piece of, a pair of, a sort of.*

Dénombrables

- Certains indénombrables (singulier de forme) sont **suivis d'un verbe au singulier**.

Exemple *jam, money, weather, music, work, luggage, furniture, advice, information…*

- Il en est de même pour certains indénombrables (pluriel de forme).

Exemple *news, means…*

Indénombrables

- Certains noms concrets (pluriel de forme) sont **suivis d'un verbe au pluriel** : *goods, trousers, pyjamas, glasses, scissors…*
- Il en est de même pour les mots *cattle, people, the police.*

Certains noms changent de **sens** au pluriel.

Exemple *cloth* (tissu), *clothes* (vêtements).

Dans les noms composés, la **marque du pluriel** ne s'applique qu'au second élément.

Exemple *boyfriends, bedrooms…* **mais :** *passers-by, lookers-on…* (le second élément ne peut porter la marque du pluriel).

S'entraîner

1 ★ Dans la liste ci-dessous, cochez les mots qui peuvent prendre la marque du pluriel.

1. ☐ noise
2. ☐ music
3. ☐ furniture
4. ☐ work
5. ☐ ham
6. ☐ sheep
7. ☐ traffic jam
8. ☐ currency
9. ☐ luck

2 ★ Dans la liste ci-dessous, cochez les noms qui peuvent être précédés de *a*/*an*.

1. ☐ information
2. ☐ mathematics
3. ☐ job
4. ☐ butter
5. ☐ time
6. ☐ women
7. ☐ experience
8. ☐ forget-me-not
9. ☐ children
10. ☐ room

3 ★★ Traduisez les phrases suivantes.

1. Ses bagages ont été livrés à l'hôtel hier.

....

2. Les meubles modernes sont appréciés par les gens pratiques.

....

3. Un bon renseignement vaut mieux qu'un bon conseil.

....

4. Les gens écoutent les informations tous les matins.

....

5. La police a constaté que les marchandises étaient abîmées.

....

Auto évaluation — Très bien ☐ Bien ☐ Pas assez bien ☐

GRAMMAIRE

34 Les quantificateurs

→ Corrigés p. IV

Observer et retenir

Helping the poorest

There are **too many** homeless people. **Many** of them sleep in the streets. **A lot of** them **don't** have **any** money. **A few of** them are rescued, but **not many** are those who accept to be helped by the police.

There is **too much** to do to help them. They need **a lot of** food and **much** care. I think **anybody** could give them **some** money and **a little** love. Would that be **enough**?

- ***Some*** s'emploie dans une affirmation ou dans une question polie.
- ***Any*** s'emploie dans une question, dans une négation (*not… any*) ou dans une affirmation (= n'importe quel).
- ***No*** s'emploie dans une négation (*no parking*). Il est accompagné d'une forme verbale affirmative (*I bought no books today*).

	dénombrables	indénombrables
+	too many	too much
	(many)	(much)
	a lot of	a lot of
	not many	not much
	a few	a little
	some	some
–	no/nothing	no/none
	Question : How many?	**How much?**
	Enough enough money, enough banknotes	

Remarque
Les composés en *-body*, *-thing*, *-one* et *-where* suivent les mêmes règles.

S'entraîner

1 ★ Complétez les phrases suivantes à l'aide des quantificateurs qui conviennent.

1. There were .... people but there was not .... applause.
(enough – a lot of – a little – much – no)

2. In fact, I can't tell .... people were present but only .... of them were satisfied.
(many – a lot of – how many – not much – a few)

3. The scene was empty and dark: there was not .... scenery and only .... light.
(much – many – a few – a little – little)

2 ★★ Complétez les phrases suivantes à l'aide de *some*, *any* ou *no* et de leurs composés.

1. .... people think he is mad. **2.** He has .... manners, he hasn't .... education. **3.** He always has .... to tell you but .... wants to listen to him. **4.** He has .... to sleep. So he sleeps .... in the streets. **5.** If .... gives him .... food, he accepts it. **6.** He is sad for he has .... home, ... friends and .... to do.

3 ★★★ Traduisez les phrases suivantes.

1. J'ai beaucoup de chance mais je n'ai pas beaucoup d'argent.

....

....

2. Quelques personnes disent qu'elles n'en ont jamais assez.

....

....

Auto évaluation — Très bien ☐ Bien ☐ Pas assez bien ☐

35 Comparatif et superlatif

→ Corrigés p. IV

Observer et retenir

Shops vs supermarkets

Ms Brown – Look! This supermarket is getting **larger and larger** every year.
Ms Black – And **more and more important**.
Ms Brown – It'll be **the biggest** in the country pretty soon.
Ms Black – Unfortunately, there are **fewer** customers in shops than ten years ago.
Ms Brown – And **less** choice.
Ms Black – That is not **the least** serious problem.
Ms Brown – You mean it's **the worst** evolution that you can imagine. I agree with you.

	adjectifs à 1 syllabe ou 2 syllabes en -y	adjectifs à 2 syllabes et plus
Comparatifs égalité	*as* + adj. + *as*	*as* + adj. + *as*
supériorité	adj. -*er* + *than*	*more* + adj. + *than*
inégalité	*not as* + adj. + *as*	*not as* + adj. + *as*
infériorité	*less* + adj. + *than*	*less* + adj. + *than*
Superlatifs supériorité	*the* + adj. -*est* + *of*/*in*	*the most* + adj. + *of*/*in*
infériorité	*the least* + adj. + *of*/*in*	*the least* + adj. + *of*/*in*

Exceptions

good → *better* → *the best*
bad → *worse* → *the worst*

- De plus en plus → *nicer and nicer – more and more pleasant.*
- De moins en moins → *less and less nice – less and less pleasant.*
- Le complément du superlatif est introduit par *in* s'il s'agit d'un lieu, par *of* dans les autres cas et par *that* pour introduire une proposition.
- *As much/many*, *not so much/many*, *more* et *less* peuvent s'employer devant des noms.

S'entraîner

1 ★★ **Faites des phrases contenant un comparatif ou un superlatif en utilisant les éléments donnés.**

1. *(supériorité)* Everest/Mont Blanc/dangerous to climb

....

....

2. *(supériorité)* the Eiffel Tower/the Empire State Building/high

....

....

3. *(supériorité)* Everest/in the world/high/mountain

....

4. *(infériorité)* city/expensive/in Europe/Warsaw

....

2 ★★★ **Traduisez.**

1. Il devient de plus en plus difficile de trouver un appartement.

....

....

2. La circulation est pire à Mexico qu'à Paris.

....

....

Auto évaluation — Très bien ☐ Bien ☐ Pas assez bien ☐

36 Accord et désaccord ; similitude et contraste

→ Corrigés p. IV

Observer et retenir

On a rainy afternoon

MARY – I don't feel like going out.
MARK – **Neither do I**. But Tony, my dog, **does**.
MARY – Bully has **the same** behaviour **as** Tony.
MARK – **Like** all dogs – and **unlike** cats. They enjoy running everywhere.
MARY – I agree. **Whereas** cats like roaming about the house.
MARK – Anyway. What about having a game? I like playing chess.
MARY – Sorry, **I don't**. I prefer Scrabble.
MARK – **So do I**. Let's play together, shall we?

Accord ou désaccord

- **Proposition affirmative** → accord : *so* + aux. (modal) + sujet (**ex. :** *I like climbing. So does Peter.*)
  → désaccord : sujet + aux. (modal) + ***not*** (**ex. :** *I like climbing. Mary doesn't.*)
- **Proposition négative** → accord : *neither* + aux. (modal) + sujet (**ex. :** *I can't ski. Neither can Peter.*)
  → désaccord : sujet + aux. (modal) (**ex. :** *I can't ski. Mary can.*)
- **Recherche d'accord** *(tags)* : voir fiche 10.

Similitude ou contraste

Similitude	Contraste
• ***Like*** + nom/pronom : *Like father, like son.* • ***as*** + adj. (cf. fiche 35) : *She is as tall as Mary.* • ***The same … as*** : *She is the same age as Mary.*	• ***Unlike*** + nom/pronom : *Unlike her brother she works hard.* • ***Whereas*** + proposition : *She works hard whereas her brother doesn't.* • ***While*** + proposition peut indiquer une simultanéité mais aussi un contraste : *While she is doing her homework, her brother is playing records.*

S'entraîner

1 ★★ **Marquez successivement, pour chaque phrase, l'accord et le désaccord de la personne indiquée.**

1. Mary has never been to Australia. What about Peter?

a. .... b. ....

2. Mary is fond of rock'n'roll. What about her brother?

a. .... b. ....

3. Mary should take a rest. What about her sister?

a. .... b. ....

4. Mary did not go on holiday last year. What about her parents?

a. .... b. ....

2 ★★★ **Réunissez les deux propositions à l'aide de *whereas* ou de *while* suivant le sens.**

1. Mary was attending a wedding. – Her husband was attending a football match.

....

2. Mary is very good at maths. – Peter is good at sports.

....

3. Cléante likes spending money. – Harpagon wants to keep it.

....

4. My father was still at work. – My mother was already on holiday.

....

Auto évaluation Très bien ☐ Bien ☐ Pas assez bien ☐

37 Le génitif

→ Corrigés p. IV

Observer et retenir

Little Red Riding Hood speaks at last

I live at **my mother's** but I very often go to **my grandmother's**. It's **a two miles' walk** but in the forest I can see **the wolf's head** behind each tree. In **yesterday's paper** they said that **a friend of my mother's** had killed one! But it is the sort of things you can read in **a children's book** and I am not afraid.

From our correspondent in Granny's stomach.

■ Le **génitif** est une forme de complément de nom. Il indique une **relation** entre deux termes. Il peut être **déterminatif** (rôle d'un déterminant) ou **générique** (rôle d'un adjectif).

■ **Marque :**
- nom singulier → *'s*
- nom pluriel irrégulier → *'s*
- nom pluriel régulier → *'*

Attention
On peut aussi utiliser un adjectif composé.
→ *a* ***two-hour*** *ride, a* ***four-mile*** *walk*

■ **Le mot portant la marque peut être :**
- un être animé → *My dog's tail* ;
- un pays, une ville → *London's inhabitants* ;
- une date, une durée, une distance → *Yesterday's newspaper, a two hours' ride, a four miles' drive.*

■ **On omet le second terme :**
- lorsqu'il s'agit de magasins, d'églises ou de mots similaires (*shop, church*)
→ *On Sundays he goes to St Paul's (cathedral).*
- lorsque le mot est déjà exprimé auparavant → *Whose computer is it? It is my sister's.* (C'est celui de ma sœur.)

S'entraîner

1 ★★ Complétez les phrases en utilisant un génitif.

1. My parents have got a car.
Yesterday I took ....

2. In my family all the children have got their bicycles.
When the weather is fine all .... are on the road.

3. The Johnsons' use a computer.
From time to time I use ....

4. Every Saturday afternoon I walk for one hour.
On Saturday afternoons, I have ....

5. When my parents are absent, my uncle invites me for the night.
I sleep at .... when my parents are absent.

2 ★★★ Traduisez en rendant le sens des ensembles soulignés par des génitifs.

1. Ne touche pas à <u>l'ordinateur de ta sœur</u>. Ce n'est pas <u>un jouet d'enfant</u>.
....

2. J'irai à <u>la fête de Mark</u> avec <u>une des amies de Mary</u>.
....

3. Ma mère va <u>chez le coiffeur</u> toutes les semaines.
....

4. Comme je n'ai pas de smartphone, j'emprunte <u>celui de mon père</u>.
....
....

Auto évaluation Très bien ☐ Bien ☐ Pas assez bien ☐

38 L'exclamation

→ Corrigés p. IV

Observer et retenir

Enthusiasm

SUE – **How lucky** I am! I'm invited to spend a month in the USA, at my cousins'.

TOM – In **such a beautiful country**! **How wonderful**!

SUE – It was **so unexpected**, you know. It is **such a good surprise**.

TOM – I'd be **so pleased** to go with you to watch **such magnificent landscapes**. **What beauty**! **What nice cousins** you've got over there!

- ***How*** + adjectif → *How nice she is!*
- ***So*** + adjectif → *She is so nice.*
- ***Such***
  - *a* + (adj.) + nom singulier dénombrable → *She is such a nice girl.*
  - Ø + (adj.) + nom pluriel dénombrable → *Such lovely flowers!*
  - Ø + (adj.) + nom indénombrable → *Such beauty!*
- ***What***
  - *a* + (adj.) + nom singulier dénombrable → *What a nice girl (she is)!*
  - Ø + (adj.) + nom pluriel dénombrable → *What lovely flowers!*
  - Ø + (adj.) + nom indénombrable → *What beauty!*
- ***So much*** + nom indénombrable → *She has so much luck.*
- ***So many*** + nom dénombrable au pluriel → *She has so many friends.*

Remarque
Pas d'inversion « sujet + verbe » dans les phrases exclamatives.
→ *How gorgeous this sight is!*

S'entraîner

1 ★ Complétez à l'aide de *so*, *such* ou *such a*.

1. She is .... nice person.
2. There is .... much noise that I can't hear you.
3. I always enjoy seeing .... good films.
4. It is a challenge to teach .... gifted children.

2 ★★ Transformez les phrases suivantes en phrases exclamatives.

Attention
Il y a deux solutions pour chaque phrase.

1. This boy is very clever.

a. ....

b. ....

2. This man looks miserable.

a. ....

b. ....

3. I've spent wonderful years abroad.

a. ....

b. ....

4. The weather is awful today.

a. ....

b. ....

3 ★★★ Traduisez sur une feuille à part.

1. Quel beau tapis ! Je n'ai jamais vu de si belles couleurs.
2. Quel talent ! Il y a tant d'amour dans ses tableaux.
3. Quelle découverte ! Mais Christophe Colomb était un si bon marin.

Auto évaluation Très bien ☐ Bien ☐ Pas assez bien ☐

Verbes irréguliers

Base verbale	Prétérit	Participe passé	Sens usuel
be	was/were	been	être
bear	bore	borne	porter, supporter
beat	beat	beaten	battre
become	became	become	devenir
begin	began	begun	commencer
bend	bent	bent	plier, courber
bet	bet	bet	parier
bite	bit	bitten	mordre
blow	blew	blown	souffler
break	broke	broken	casser
bring	brought	brought	apporter, amener
broadcast	broadcast	broadcast	diffuser
build	built	built	construire
burn	burnt	burnt	brûler
burst	burst	burst	éclater
buy	bought	bought	acheter
catch	caught	caught	attraper
choose	chose	chosen	choisir
come	came	come	venir
cost	cost	cost	coûter
cut	cut	cut	couper
deal	dealt	dealt	traiter, distribuer
dig	dug	dug	creuser
do	did	done	faire
draw	drew	drawn	dessiner
dream	dreamt	dreamt	rêver
drink	drank	drunk	boire
drive	drove	driven	conduire
eat	ate	eaten	manger
fall	fell	fallen	tomber
feed	fed	fed	nourrir
feel	felt	felt	sentir
fight	fought	fought	battre
find	found	found	trouver
fly	flew	flown	voler
forbid	forbade	forbidden	interdire
forget	forgot	forgotten	oublier
forgive	forgave	forgiven	pardonner
freeze	froze	frozen	geler
get	got	got	obtenir
give	gave	given	donner
go	went	gone	aller
grow	grew	grown	pousser, faire pousser, grandir
hang	hung	hung	suspendre, pendre
have	had	had	avoir
hear	heard	heard	entendre
hide	hid	hidden	(se) cacher
hit	hit	hit	frapper
hold	held	held	tenir
hurt	hurt	hurt	faire mal, blesser
keep	kept	kept	garder
know	knew	known	savoir
lead	led	led	mener
leave	left	left	laisser, quitter

Base verbale	Prétérit	Participe passé	Sens usuel
lend	lent	lent	prêter
let	let	let	laisser, permettre
lie	lay	lain	être étendu
light	lit	lit	éclairer, allumer
lose	lost	lost	perdre
make	made	made	faire
mean	meant	meant	vouloir dire, signifier
meet	met	met	rencontrer
mow	mowed	mown	tondre
pay	paid	paid	payer
put	put	put	mettre
read	read	read	lire
rent	rent	rent	louer
ride	rode	ridden	aller à vélo, monter (cheval, etc.)
ring	rang	rung	sonner
run	ran	run	courir
say	said	said	dire
see	saw	seen	voir
sell	sold	sold	vendre
send	sent	sent	envoyer
set	set	set	poser, placer
shake	shook	shaken	secouer
shine	shone	shone	briller
shoot	shot	shot	tirer (arme à feu)
show	showed	shown	montrer
shut	shut	shut	fermer
sing	sang	sung	chanter
sink	sank	sunk	sombrer
sit	sat	sat	être assis
sleep	slept	slept	dormir
slide	slid	slid	glisser
smell	smelt	smelt	sentir (odorat)
speak	spoke	spoken	parler
spend	spent	spent	dépenser, passer (du temps)
spill	spilt	spilt	répandre
spoil	spoilt	spoilt	gâcher, abîmer
spread	spread	spread	(se) répandre, étaler
stand	stood	stood	être debout
steal	stole	stolen	voler (dérober)
stick	stuck	stuck	coller
sting	stung	stung	piquer
strike	struck	struck	frapper
swear	swore	sworn	jurer
sweep	swept	swept	balayer
swim	swam	swum	nager
take	took	taken	prendre
teach	taught	taught	enseigner
tear	tore	torn	déchirer
tell	told	told	dire, raconter
think	thought	thought	penser
throw	threw	thrown	jeter/lancer
understand	understood	understood	comprendre
wake up	woke up	woken up	(se) réveiller
wear	wore	worn	porter
win	won	won	gagner
write	wrote	written	écrire

Constructions prépositionnelles

Verbes

about → *worry about:* s'inquiéter de/pour
after → *look after:* s'occuper de
at → *laugh at:* se moquer de
look at: regarder
back → *date back to:* remonter à (temps)
for → *apologise for:* s'excuser de
apply for: postuler à (une offre d'emploi)
blame somebody for something: reprocher quelque chose à quelqu'un
care for sth: aimer quelque chose
hope for: espérer
long for: désirer vivement
look for: chercher
sit for (an exam): se présenter à
wait for: attendre
from → *borrow sth from somebody:* emprunter quelque chose à quelqu'un
hear from somebody: avoir des nouvelles de quelqu'un
prevent somebody from doing something: empêcher quelqu'un de faire quelque chose
steal sth from somebody: voler quelque chose à quelqu'un
in → *participate in something:* participer à
into → *break into:* cambrioler
like → *feel like:* avoir envie de
look like: ressembler à
sound like: ressembler à (son)
taste like: ressembler à (goût)
of → *accuse of:* accuser de
approve of: approuver
complain of/about: se plaindre de
dream of: rêver de
(be) fond of: aimer, apprécier
hear of: entendre parler de
remind somebody of something: rappeler quelque chose à quelqu'un
take care of: s'occuper de
think of/about: penser à
on → *comment on:* commenter
depend on: dépendre de
get on/off: monter/descendre (d'un bus/train)

Attention

Certains verbes qui, en français, sont suivis d'une préposition se construisent sans préposition en anglais :

- ***answer:*** répondre à
- ***obey:*** obéir à
- ***remember:*** se souvenir de

to → *belong to:* appartenir à
listen to: écouter
look forward to: attendre impatiemment
with → *agree with:* être d'accord avec
deal with: traiter (un sujet)

Adjectifs

about → *crazy about:* fou de
at → *angry at:* fâché à propos de
good at: bon en
surprised at: surpris de
for → *responsible for:* responsable de
sorry for: désolé de
from → *different from:* différent de
in → *interested in:* intéressé par
of → *aware of:* conscient de
capable of: capable de
proud of: fier de
tired of: fatigué de
on → *keen on:* passionné de
to → *contrary to:* contraire à
eager to: désireux de
kind to: aimable envers/avec
similar to: semblable à
with → *angry with:* fâché contre quelqu'un
busy with: occupé à
disappointed with: déçu de
pleased with: content de

Verbes à particule

back

answer back: répondre impoliment
come back: revenir
go back: rentrer, retourner
hand back: rendre (un devoir)
look back: se retourner

down

break down: avoir une panne, faire une dépression
burn down: détruire par le feu
go down: descendre
pull down: démolir
sit down: s'asseoir

in

come in: entrer
move in: emménager

off

put off: remettre, reporter une réunion…
take off: retirer un vêtement, décoller (avion)
turn off: éteindre (TV, gaz)

on

call on: rendre visite à
get on with: s'entendre avec
go on: continuer, poursuivre
put on: mettre un vêtement
try on: essayer un vêtement
turn on: allumer (TV, gaz)
wait on: servir quelqu'un

out

blow out: souffler (bougies)
break out: éclater (guerre, orage)
find out: découvrir
Look out!: Attention !
move out: déménager
wear out: user

over

run over: écraser, renverser

round

show round: faire visiter

up

bring up: élever (un enfant)
clear up: dégager (un espace, un lieu), s'éclaircir (temps)
give up: renoncer à
make up one's mind: se décider
pick up: cueillir (fleur), prendre quelqu'un dans sa voiture
ring up: téléphoner
set up (a business): monter une affaire
stand up: se lever
sum up: résumer
wake up: (se) réveiller
be fed up with: en avoir assez de
put up with: tolérer
It's up to you: À vous de voir
Speak up: Parlez (plus) fort !

Lexique

La traduction indiquée correspond au sens des mots rencontrés dans les exercices.

A

a few: quelques
a lot of: beaucoup de
a, an: un(e)
abroad: à l'étranger
absent-minded: distrait
accuse of: accuser de
acquire: acquérir
ad: publicité
addict: fanatique
admirer: admirateur
advice: conseils
aerial: antenne (TV)
afford: se payer
afraid: effrayé
ago: il y a (temps)
agree with: être d'accord avec
allowed to (be): (être) autorisé à
almost: presque
already: déjà
although: bien que
angel: ange
angry: en colère
angry at: fâché à propos de
angry with: fâché contre quelqu'un
another: un(e) autre
answer: répondre à
answer back: répondre impoliment
anthem: hymne national
any: du, de la, des (négatif, interrogatif), n'importe quel
anybody: quelqu'un (négatif, interrogatif), n'importe qui
anyway: en tout cas
apologise for: s'excuser de
applause: applaudissements
applicant: candidat (emploi)
application form: formulaire
apply: appliquer (la loi)
apply for: postuler à (une offre d'emploi)
appoint: nommer (emploi)
appointment: rendez-vous (docteur, etc.)
approve of: approuver
as: en tant que
as soon as: aussitôt que
as usual: comme d'habitude
at last: enfin
at least: au moins
attend: assister à
audience: le public
aunt: tante
author: auteur
aware of: conscient de
awful: horrible
awkward: maladroit

B

bachelor: célibataire (homme)
backpack: sac à dos
ballot box: urne (vote)
ballot paper: bulletin de vote
ban: interdire, bannir
bark: aboyer
barn: grange
barrister: avocat
battered: cabossé
bear (v. i.)**:** supporter
become (v. i.)**:** devenir
before: avant (que)
beg: mendier
begin (v. i.)**:** commencer
behaviour: comportement
believe: croire
belong to: appartenir à
better: mieux
bill: projet de loi
birth: naissance
birthday: anniversaire
blame somebody for something: reprocher quelque chose à quelqu'un
blow out: souffler (bougie)
board: conseil d'administration
board: embarquer
boarding card: carte d'embarquement
boil: bouillir
borrow something from somebody: emprunter quelque chose à quelqu'un
bossy: autoritaire
bottom: bas (hauteur)
break down (v. i.)**:** avoir une panne, faire une dépression
break into: cambrioler
break out: éclater (orage, guerre)
bright: brillant
bring up (v. i.)**:** élever (enfant)
build (v. i.)**:** construire
bump: tamponner, heurter
burglar: cambrioleur
burn down (v. i.)**:** détruire par le feu
burst in (v. i.)**:** faire irruption
bury: enterrer
busy with: occupé à, chargé de
but: ne… que
butter: beurre
by: par, près de
by now: à l'heure actuelle
by the way: à propos

C

call on: rendre visite à
campsite: camping
cancel: annuler
capable of: capable de
care: soin, attention
care for something: aimer quelque chose
careful: prudent
careful (be): faire attention
carefully: soigneusement
careless: négligent
carry: porter, transporter
castle: château
cattle: bétail
chairman: président (société)
challenge: défi
cheat: tricher, tromper
cherry: cerise
chess: les échecs (jeu)
china: porcelaine
choice: choix
choir: chœur
choose (v. i.)**:** choisir
church: église
churchyard: cimetière
citizen: citoyen
clean: nettoyer
clear up: dégager (un espace), s'éclaircir (temps)
clerk: employé
clever: astucieux, malin
climb up: faire l'ascension de

clothes: vêtements
cloud: nuage
clumsy: maladroit
coin: pièce (de monnaie)
college: établissement d'enseignement supérieur
come back: revenir
come in: entrer
comment on: commenter
company: société, entreprise
compel: obliger à
complain of/about: se plaindre de
complete: terminer, achever
computer: ordinateur
conductor: chef d'orchestre
contrary to: contraire à
convince: convaincre
cost (v. i.)**:** coûter
country: campagne, pays
country people: les ruraux
cow: vache
crazy about: fou de
crime: délit
crisis: crise
cross: furieux
cross: croix
cross: traverser (rue)
crossroads: croisement
cry: pleurer
currency: monnaie, devise
customer: client

D

daffodil: jonquille
damage: endommager, abîmer
dark: sombre, noir
date back to: remonter à (temps)
daughter-in-law: belle-fille
dead: mort
deal with: traiter (un sujet)
dedicate: consacrer
deep: profond
delay: retarder
delighted: enchanté, ravi
deliver: livrer, distribuer
demonstration: manifestation
depend on: dépendre de
desk: bureau (meuble)
Devil: le Diable
different from: différent de
dirty: sale
disappointed with: déçu de
discover: découvrir
dismiss: renvoyer (emploi)
dissolve: dissoudre
do one's best: faire de son mieux
dole: allocation de chômage
dolphin: dauphin
double-decker: bus à étage
dream of (v. i.)**:** rêver de, à
dress: robe
drive: allée
drive (v. i.)**:** conduire (voiture)
driving licence: permis de conduire
dull: terne (couleur)
dump: décharge (ordures)
duty: devoir (moral)

E

eager to: très désireux de
early: tôt, de bonne heure
Earth: terre
Earthmen: les terriens
earthquake: tremblement de terre
easy: facile
efficient: efficace
either ... or: soit ... soit
elect: élire
else: autre
employee: employé
empty: vide
endanger: menacer de disparition
enjoy: prendre plaisir à, profiter de
enough: assez (de)
entertainment: distraction, loisir
enthusiastic: enthousiaste
environmentalist: écologiste
evening: soir
every: chaque
everywhere: partout
excited: agité
exclaim: s'exclamer
executive: cadre (entreprise)
exhausted: épuisé
expect: s'attendre à (ce que)
expensive: cher, coûteux
explain: expliquer

F

factory: usine
fair-haired: blond(e)
faithful: fidèle
fallout: retombées (nucléaires)
far: loin
farm: une ferme
fast: rapide
fatal: mortel
father-in-law: beau-père
feature: trait (visage, caractère)
fed up with (be) (v. i.)**:** en avoir assez de
feel like: avoir envie de
feeling: sentiment
fence: barrière
fertiliser: engrais
find (v. i.)**:** trouver
find out: découvrir
fire: mettre à la porte
firm: entreprise, société
first: d'abord
first cousin: cousin germain
fish: pêcher
flag: drapeau
flat: appartement
flight: vol (avion)
flood: inondation
flu: la grippe
fluently: couramment
fly (v. i.)**:** voyager en avion
fond of (be): aimer, apprécier
food: nourriture
for: pendant
for ages: depuis fort longtemps
forbid (v. i.)**:** interdire
foreman: contremaître
forget (v. i.)**:** oublier
formerly: autrefois
fortunately: heureusement
free: libre
frighten: faire peur, effrayer
full: plein
furniture: le mobilier

G

gale: rafale de vent
gambling: le jeu (d'argent)
game: jeu
get on sb's nerves: énerver quelqu'un
get on with (v. i.)**:** s'entendre avec
get on/off (v. i.)**:** monter/descendre (bus, train…)
ghost: fantôme
gift: cadeau, don
gifted: doué
give up: renoncer à
glad: content
glasses: lunettes
glue: coller
go back: rentrer, retourner
go down: descendre
go on: continuer, poursuivre
God: Dieu

good at: bon en
goods: marchandises
gorgeous: magnifique
grandchildren: petits-enfants
grasp: saisir
greenhouse: serre (plantes)
ground: sol, terrain
grow (v. i.)**:** pousser, grandir
grown up: adulte
guess: deviner
guilty: coupable

H

ham: jambon
hand back: rendre (devoir)
happen: arriver, se produire, avoir lieu
hard: dur
hat: chapeau
hate: détester
haunted: hanté
health: santé
healthy: sain
hear from somebody (v. i.)**:** avoir des nouvelles de quelqu'un
hear of (v. i.)**:** entendre parler de
heatwave: vague de chaleur
heaven: paradis
heavy: lourd
hedge: haie
hell: enfer
help (I can't): empêcher de (je ne peux m')
help: aider
help oneself with: se servir de (nourriture)
hire: embaucher
hit (v. i.)**:** frapper
hitchhike: faire de l'auto-stop
hole: trou
homeless: sans abri
honours (with): mention (avec)
hope for: espérer
how: comme (exclamatif)
how much/many: combien
hurry up: se dépêcher
hurt (v. i.)**:** blesser, faire mal
husband: mari

I

ill: malade
ill-at-ease: mal à l'aise
income: le revenu
increase: augmenter
information: renseignements
inhabitant: habitant
inside: à l'intérieur (de)
insurance: assurance (vie…)
interested in: intéressé par
introduce sb to sb: présenter quelqu'un à quelqu'un
isle, island: île
it's up to you: à vous de voir

J

jam: confiture
jealous: jaloux
Jew: juif
jewel: bijou
jewish: juif
job centre: agence pour l'emploi
jobless: sans emploi
jump: sauter

K

keen on: passionné de
key: clé
keyboard: clavier
kill: tuer
kind to: aimable envers/avec
knock: frapper

L

land: accoster, atterrir
landscape: paysage
lane: sentier
large: grand, spacieux
late: en retard
laugh at: se moquer de
launch: lancer (fusée)
launderette: laverie automatique
laundry: le linge sale
law: loi, le droit
lawyer: homme de loi
layer: couche
lead-free: sans plomb
leak: fuite (eau…)
leave (v. i.)**:** partir, laisser, quitter
leek: poireau
leisure: les loisirs
lie: mentir
life: vie
light: lumière
like: comme (comparaison)
lily of the valley: muguet
listen to: écouter
live: habiter, vivre
long: longtemps
long for: désirer vivement
look after: s'occuper de
look at: regarder
look back: se retourner
look down on: mépriser
look for: chercher
look forward to: attendre avec impatience
look like: ressembler à
look out!: attention !
look up in: chercher dans (dico)
loud: fort (son, bruit)
luck: chance
lucky: chanceux
luggage: bagages
lung: poumon

M

mad: fou
magnificent: magnifique
make up one's mind: se décider
manage: diriger
manager: directeur
manners: manières (éducation)
many: beaucoup de (pluriel)
map: carte, plan
marry sb: épouser quelqu'un
material: matériau
meadow: pré, prairie
meal: repas
mean (v. i.)**:** vouloir dire
means: moyen
meat: viande
midday: midi
mind (I don't): ça m'est égal
mind (to my): à mon avis
miserable: malheureux
miss: manquer
mix: mélanger
moped: mobylette
mother-in-law: belle-mère
motorway: autoroute
mouth: embouchure (fleuve)
move: bouger
move in: emménager
move out: déménager
moved: ému
much: beaucoup de (singulier)
Muslim: musulman

N

nasty: méchant
nasty words: gros mots

national service: service militaire
naughty: méchant, pas sage
nearly: presque
need: avoir besoin de
neighbour: voisin
neither: ni, non plus
nephew: neveu
news: nouvelles, informations
newsagent: vendeur de journaux
newspaper: journal
no: non, ne... pas, aucun
noise: bruit
no... longer: ne... plus
none: aucun
nothing: rien
notice board: panneau d'affichage
novelist: romancier
nowadays: actuellement
nuisance (make a - of oneself): se rendre désagréable

O

obey: obéir à
obstinacy: obstination
occur: arriver (évènement)
of course: bien sûr
off duty: pas de service
office: bureau (pièce)
oil slick: marée noire
on duty: de service
once: une fois
order: ordonner, commander
outing: sortie, promenade
outside: dehors, à l'extérieur de
over: terminé

P

pack: faire ses bagages
paint: peindre
painting: tableau (art)
pane: vitre
paper: devoir (classe)
participate in something: participer à
party: fête
pass: réussir à (un examen)
passer-by: passant, piéton
past: passé
pattern: motif (art)
performance: représentation
petrol: essence
pick up: cueillir (fleur), prendre quelqu'un dans sa voiture
pilgrim: pèlerin
pious: pieux
pitch: terrain (de sport)
place: lieu, endroit
plan: organiser
pleased with: content de, satisfait de
policy: police (assurance)
polling day: jour des élections
pollute: polluer
poppy: coquelicot
pour: tomber à verse
power: puissance
practise: pratiquer (sport)
pray: prier
preacher: prédicateur
prejudiced against (be): avoir des préjugés envers
pretty: assez, plutôt
prevent somebody from doing something: empêcher quelqu'un de faire quelque chose
previous: précédent
priest: prêtre
promise: promettre
properly: convenablement
properties: affaires personnelles
prosecution: accusation
proud of: fier de
pull down: démolir
put off (v. i.)**:** remettre, reporter (une réunion)
put on (v. i.)**:** mettre (vêtement)
put up with: tolérer
puzzled: perplexe

Q

quiet: calme, silence

R

race: course
rain: pleuvoir
rainy: pluvieux
rate: tarif
rather: plutôt
ready: prêt
realise: se rendre compte
receive: recevoir
record: disque
recover: se remettre, guérir
reliable: sûr, de confiance
relieved: soulagé
remains: restes
remember: se rappeler
remind somebody of something: rappeler quelque chose à quelqu'un
rent: louer (appartement, auto)
replace: remplacer
reply: répliquer
report: rapporter (un fait...)
rescue: sauver
responsible for: responsable de
rest: se reposer
resume: reprendre (travail)
retire: prendre sa retraite
retired: retraité
retirement: retraite
reward: récompenser
rewarding: gratifiant
ride: trajet, parcours (auto)
right (be): avoir raison
ring up (v. i.)**:** téléphoner à
risky: risqué
road: route
roam: errer, traîner (dans les rues)
rocket: fusée
room: pièce, espace
route: itinéraire
rubbish: ordures
rude: grossier, impoli
ruin: détruire
ruler: règle (objet)
run over (v. i.)**:** écraser, renverser

S

sack: licencier
sail: naviguer
sailor: marin
same: même (égalité)
satellite dish: parabole (TV)
save: économiser, sauver
scenery: décor
scissors: ciseaux
score: marquer (but)
scornful: méprisant
seaside: bord de mer
selfish: égoïste
sell (v. i.)**:** vendre
semi-detached: jumelé
sensible: raisonnable
sentence: condamner
set up (a business) (v. i.)**:** monter une affaire
settle: s'installer
shamrock: trèfle
sheep: mouton
sheet: couche
shine (v. i.)**:** briller (astre...)
shout: crier
show round (v. i.)**:** faire visiter

shy: timide
sight: vue
sightseeing: tourisme
silent: silencieux
silly: stupide
similar to: semblable à
since: depuis
sit down (v. i.)**:** s'asseoir
sit for (an exam) (v. i.)**:** se présenter à (un examen)
skilled: qualifié
sleep (v. i.)**:** dormir
slim: mince (personne)
sloppy: négligé, débraillé
so: aussi, tellement, si
society: la société
sock: chaussette
soft: mou
some: du, de la, des (positif)
soon: bientôt
sorry for: désolé de
sound like: ressembler à (son)
space: espace
space station: station spatiale
spacecraft: vaisseau spatial
spaceman: astronaute
speak up!: parlez (plus) fort !
species: espèce
spend (v. i.)**:** passer (du temps)
spill (v. i.)**:** répandre, renverser
spoil (v. i.)**:** gâcher, abîmer
spray: aérosol
spray: vaporiser
stain: tache
stand up (v. i.)**:** se lever
Star-Spangled Banner: La Bannière étoilée
start: débuter
stay: séjourner
steal something from somebody (v. i.)**:** voler, dérober quelque chose à quelqu'un
steeple: clocher
still: encore
storey: étage
storm: tempête
street lights: feux tricolores
strike: grève
stubborn: entêté
study: étudier
succeed: réussir
successful: prospère
such: si, tel(les)
suggest: suggérer
suitcase: valise
sum up: résumer
sunset: coucher de soleil
surprised at: surpris de
surround: entourer
swear (v. i.)**:** jurer
swim (v. i.)**:** nager
swimsuit: maillot de bain
switch on: allumer (TV, lampe…)

T

tail: queue
take advantage of: profiter de
take care of: s'occuper de
take off (v. i.)**:** retirer (vêtement), décoller (avion)
take out: sortir (animal…)
take place: avoir lieu, se passer
talk: conversation
talkative: bavard
tall: grand
tanker: pétrolier (navire)
taste like: ressembler à (goût)
team: équipe
that: qui, que
the: le, la, les
thin: mince
think of/about (v. i.)**:** penser à
thistle: chardon
threaten: menacer
time: fois
tired: fatigué
tombstone: pierre tombale
tonight: ce soir
too: trop
top: haut
tower: tour
town dweller: citadin
toy: jouet
trade unionist: syndicaliste
traffic jam: embouteillage
trainer: formateur
training course: stage
tramp: clochard
translate: traduire
travel agent: voyagiste
trial: procès
trip: voyage
trousers: pantalon
truth: vérité
try: essai
try: essayer
try on: essayer (vêtement)
tune (in): juste (musique)
turn off: éteindre (TV, gaz…)
turn on: allumer (TV, gaz…)
turn out: devenir
twice: deux fois
type: taper à la machine

U

umbrella: parapluie
uncle: oncle
unemployed: au chômage
unemployment: chômage
unexpected: inattendu
unfortunately: malheureusement
unlike: à la différence de
unpleasant: désagréable
unskilled: sans qualification
until: jusqu'à (ce que)
upset: bouleversé
use: se servir de
used to (be): avoir l'habitude de

V

vacation (US): vacances
vexed: vexé, blessé

W

wages: salaire
wait for: attendre
wait on: servir (quelqu'un)
wake up (v. i.)**:** (se) réveiller
walk: promenade
wash: baigner, laver
waste: déchets
watch: montre
watch: regarder, observer
way: façon, manière
wear out (v. i.)**:** user
weather: temps (atmosphérique)
wedding: mariage (cérémonie)
wet: mouillé, humide
what: qu'est-ce que, quel(le) (exclamatif)
when: quand
where: où
whereas: tandis que
which: qui, que
while: pendant que
who: qui (personne)
whose: dont
why: pourquoi
widow: veuve
wife: femme, épouse
wish: souhait
wish: souhaiter
witness: témoin
wolf: loup

wonder: se demander
wonderful: merveilleux
work: fonctionner, marcher
worker: ouvrier, travailleur
workman: ouvrier
world: le monde, l'univers
worried: inquiet, ennuyé
worry about: s'inquiéter de
worse: pire
worship: adorer (Dieu...)
worth (be): valoir la peine
wrecked (be): faire naufrage

Y

yet (not... yet): pas encore
youth: jeunesse, jeune homme, jeune fille

Certifié PEFC
Ce produit est issu de forêts gérées durablement et de sources contrôlées
PEFC
PEFC/18-31-264
www.pefc-france.org

Achevé d'imprimer en novembre 2020
par «La Tipografica Varese Srl» en Italie
N° éditeur : MAGSI20200954
Dépôt légal : janvier 2019

IMPRIM'VERT
Votre imprimeur agit pour l'environnement